MAGIC & MISDEEDS

STARRY HOLLOW WITCHES, BOOK 11

ANNABEL CHASE

RED PALM PRESS LLC

CHAPTER ONE

ARE we out of breadsticks again? Raoul complained. My raccoon familiar raided the pantry while I made a pitcher of homemade dandelion iced tea. I contemplated adding a splash or five of vodka to liven up my little get-together but, surprisingly, common sense prevailed.

"What do you mean *again*?" I asked. "I don't remember opening the last box."

He vacated the pantry and climbed onto the island. *I think I saw Marley with suspicious crumbs on her face last night.*

I gave him a long look. "Are you sure it wasn't your own reflection in the mirror?"

Raoul licked his paws and smoothed back his fur. *It's hard to mistake this model of perfection for anyone else.*

He sprawled across the island like he was preparing for a photo shoot and I shooed him away. "Get down before you get fur in the iced tea."

For someone who regularly extends the five-second rule to sixty, you're being awfully particular.

I narrowed my eyes at him. "I don't think my cousins will appreciate a dash of raccoon in their drinks."

Because they're snobs. Everybody knows raccoon hair is a delicacy.

"They're not snobs," I said hotly. "Maybe Aunt Hyacinth is, but Florian and Aster are very down-to-earth." As far as privileged wizards and witches went, I'd lucked out with the younger generation of Rose-Muldoons.

Before the doorbell even rang, my aging Yorkshire terrier —Prescott Peabody III—began to bark from his place on the sofa like a murderer was climbing through the window.

"Calm down," I scolded him as I passed by. "It's just Florian and Aster." I opened the door to greet my cousins.

"Hello there." Aster kissed my cheek as she entered.

PP3 gave one more half-hearted growl before settling back down on the sofa. "Come on in," I said. "Don't let the guard dog put you off."

"Mr. Peabody and I are old pals, aren't we?" Florian walked to the sofa to scratch the dog's head.

"I had a nosy peek at your herb garden outside," Aster said. "It's coming along nicely."

"You can credit Marley for that," I said. "I've found it best to keep well away so I can't be blamed for anything that goes wrong."

"A reasonable plan," Florian said. He removed his sunglasses and I noticed his bloodshot eyes.

"Late night?" I asked, with a trace of amusement.

He grinned. "Aren't they all?"

I motioned for them to sit and took my place beside the dog. "Thanks for meeting me here. I've got to run Marley straight to her music lesson after school, so the window of opportunity is short."

Aster perched on the edge of the chair opposite me. "Mother mentioned that you're covering this weekend's Wizards Connect tournament for the paper, so we thought we should give you all the background information before it starts." Aster's gaze darted to her brother. "We know your technological skills are somewhat…"

"Lacking? Nonexistent?" I waved a hand. "It's fine. You can say it. I know what my limitations are."

Are you sure about that? Raoul asked, joining us around the coffee table. *I've seen you inhale a whole pepperoni pizza.*

I glared at the raccoon. *Can you not critique me while I'm hosting? It's distracting.*

His beady eyes widened. *Oh, this is hosting?* He surveyed the room in an exaggerated fashion. *Heavens to Betsy. Wherever are the crudités?*

I made iced tea. Oh. "I made iced tea," I announced hastily. "Let me get it." I hurried toward the kitchen.

"Anything that involves hydration is probably a good idea for me," Florian called after me.

I was relieved that I chose the responsible path and omitted the vodka. I poured two glasses and returned to the living area to hand one to each of my guests. I'd never be Martha Stewart, but I was okay with that.

"So, what do I need to know about this tournament?" I asked.

Florian lit up. "It's going to be amazing. Paranormals are already flocking to town. I went into the Whitethorn last night and it was positively heaving."

I arched an eyebrow. "Really? Aren't these losers…I mean, these gamers all introverts?"

"Not all," Florian said. "I met a pixie last night in town for the tournament who would definitely qualify as extroverted."

Aster groaned. "I think you're confusing extrovert with hyperextended."

"I'll show you the game," Florian said. He tapped his phone and showed me the screen. "For purposes of the tournament, all you need to know is that whichever gamer obtains the Emerald Chalice first is the winner."

"What do they win?" I asked.

Florian's brow wrinkled in confusion. "A trophy that looks like the Emerald Chalice and bragging rights, of course."

"No money?" I asked.

Not even free pizza? Raoul blew a raspberry. *I was going to find an old phone at the dump so I could play, but sounds like it's not worth it.*

"They play because they love the game and this is an opportunity to get together with other like-minded individuals," Aster explained. "They'll build friendships that can last a lifetime."

Raoul pretended to snore.

"A geek fest," I said. "I get it."

Florian started swiping on his screen and I gasped as he staked a vampire. "Got him," he said, and pumped his fist in the air.

"Why did you have to kill him?" I asked.

Florian looked at me. "You know he isn't real, right? It's not like I just murdered your boyfriend."

"Killing paranormals is part of the game," Aster said. "They present as obstacles to your goals. Vampires are one of the hardest to kill."

Naturally.

"Leprechauns are the easiest," Florian said. "You use one of the iron items in your supply list and bam!" He grinned. "Is it wrong that I laugh whenever I kill one? They make these angry faces right before they die, like they're so affronted that you killed them."

I squinted at the screen. "What kind of supplies do you have?"

He tapped the screen to open to a new page and pointed. "You collect things you find as you go because you never know what will come in handy. I'm a fan of the silver lasso and the cast iron skillet because they're useful for both killing and survival skills."

"Or you can buy them with gold," Aster said.

"Why would the lasso be silver...?" I trailed off, the realization dawning on me. "And werewolves play this too?"

"Werewolves are a huge percentage of the WC community," Florian said.

PP3 growled at the mention of werewolves and I patted his head reassuringly. "You're not as deaf as you pretend to be, are you?"

Aster gave PP3 a disapproving look. "I'm glad we haven't given in to the boys' pleas for a dog," she said. "Cats are far less work."

"Well, we've got one of those too," I said. Sort of. Marley's familiar was a kitten—with wings. "Bonkers is young and spry, so she doesn't need the same kind of attention that PP3 does."

Does that mean when I'm old, you'll finally pay attention to me? Raoul asked.

I rolled my eyes. *Oh, right. Because you're sorely lacking in that department.*

The door burst open and Marley dragged herself into the cottage with her backpack hanging off her shoulder.

"Tough day at the office, sweetheart?" I asked. "Should I fix you a bourbon on the rocks and rub your feet?"

Marley flung the backpack against the wall and released a breath. "I have so much homework this weekend."

Florian frowned. "I thought we'd asked the schools to go easy on homework this weekend to allow for more children to participate in the tournament."

Marley laughed. "Do you really think the teachers at the Black Cloak Academy are going to withhold homework so that I can play a game on my phone all weekend?"

"In the interest of community spirit, yes," Florian said.

Marley threw herself on the sofa. "I don't want to play anyway. I'm not really into those kinds of games."

"But Wizards Connect is hugely popular," Florian said. "I'll bet lots of your friends are playing."

"I don't like that it's called Wizards Connect," Marley said. "That's so sexist. Do they assume girls aren't gaming?"

"Because Witches and Wizards Connect is presumably a mouthful," Aster said. "They want to keep it simple for marketing purposes."

"Then why not Witches Connect?" she asked.

"Because then boys probably wouldn't play," Florian said.

Marley glanced up at him. "See? Sexist."

"They should have called it Paranormals Connect," Aster said. "The game consists of all sorts of species."

"Yes, but you're playing as a wizard," Florian said. "You kill the other species in pursuit of your goal."

"I want to play," Marley announced.

"But you don't even like gaming," I protested. "You just said so."

"I've decided I want to win," she said. "I want to show them that girls can play the game every bit as well as boys." She fixed her big blue eyes on me. "Will you help me?"

I barked a short laugh. "You realize who you're asking, right?"

"The woman who short circuits the microwave," Marley said. "Yes, I'm aware. I've been living with you my whole life."

I hesitated. "You said you have a lot of homework this weekend."

"I'll manage," she said. "You know I always get my work done."

"You're already covering the tournament for the newspaper," Florian said. "Might as well immerse yourself in the topic."

I gave Marley's chin an affectionate pinch. "You know I can't resist this face."

Florian flattened his hands on his thighs. "The tournament kicks off at sunrise. The diehards won't miss it, so up to you if you want the full experience."

"So I have between now and sunrise tomorrow to learn how to play this game?" I said.

"We'll get started straight after my music lesson," Marley said.

"Not so fast," I said. "Don't forget we're going to Palmetto House for dinner."

Marley gave our cousins a deadpan look. "She never forgets a dinner when she doesn't have to cook."

"Gee, thanks," I said.

"I'll be interested to hear what you think of cousin Philip," Aster said.

"I'm interested to see what *I* think of cousin Philip," Florian said. "I haven't seen him since I was a child."

"Somehow it doesn't surprise me that he's a gamer," Aster said.

I balked. "Wait, that's why he's in town?"

"Yes," Aster said. "He's participating in the tournament."

I laughed. "Sweet baby Elvis. I thought that was a coincidence."

"You'll understand better when you meet him," Aster said.

"Have you seen him yet?" I asked.

"No, we'll be seeing him at dinner tonight, same as you," Florian said.

"Why isn't he staying with Aunt Hyacinth?" Marley asked. "She has all those extra rooms."

Aster and Florian exchanged glances. "He and Mother don't really get along," Aster said. "It's one of the reasons he hasn't been back to visit."

"He and our father were close growing up, but they grew

7

apart as they got older," Florian said. "Cousin Philip was always a bit of a free spirit. Did what he wanted and didn't mind what anyone's opinion was."

"Like you," Marley said to him.

"Not exactly." Florian patted her head. "You'll see."

Thanks to Marley's music lesson running ten minutes past schedule, we arrived late to dinner at Palmetto House. Everyone was already gathered around the table, including Linnea's kids —Bryn and Hudson—and a few guests of the inn. Linnea sometimes had the family dine in a separate area, but she must've decided to group us together tonight because of Philip's visit.

"Ember and Marley, I'd like you meet our cousin, Philip Muldoon," Linnea said.

When the wizard stood to shake my hand, it took every ounce of self-control I possessed not to react. My cousins weren't kidding about him. In a Pokémon T-shirt and faded jeans, Philip looked sixty going on sixteen.

"What an absolute pleasure," he said. "I've heard so much about you both."

"It's great to meet you," I said.

"And these are guests of the inn," Linnea continued. "Lewis and Clark are here for the tournament." She gestured to the gnome and leprechaun at the table.

"Lewis and Clark," Marley repeated. "Really?"

They exchanged baffled looks. "Yes, why?" Lewis queried.

"They're a famous pair of explorers in human history," Marley said. She took her seat beside me. "They traveled more than eight thousand miles together."

"Lewis and I have probably traveled more than eight thousand miles together at this point," the leprechaun said. "We've known each other since we were kids."

"We travel for gaming tournaments a few times a year," Lewis added.

"This is Starry Hollow's first time hosting anything like it," Linnea said. "And we've got a full house to show for it. It's going to be a busy weekend."

"We'll be out of your hair most of the time," Clark said. "We need to find all the hot spots." The leprechaun stared intently at his phone as he spoke.

"Mom, you always say no technology at the table," Hudson complained.

"And I'm making an exception this weekend for obvious reasons," Linnea replied. "Palmetto House itself is some kind of hot spot, so gamers keep appearing outside. I guess I have my siblings to thank for that." She gave Aster and Florian a pointed look.

"One was peeking in the window from the backyard earlier," Bryn said. "It was creepy."

"I thought you'd appreciate the free marketing," Florian said. "If it takes seven times for an ad to register, imagine how many times you have to see Palmetto House before deciding you might want to stay here."

"I don't think they're seeing anything beyond their phone screens," Linnea said, "but I appreciate the thought."

"It's a wonderful place you have here," Philip said. "I can imagine what your mother thinks of it though. I remember this place before you bought it. It was a fixer upper, wasn't it?"

Linnea suppressed a smile. "Yes, Mother wasn't what I would call pleased."

"Is she ever?" Philip asked.

"You do plan to see her, don't you?" Aster asked. "I think she'd be offended if you didn't at least pop in for a quick visit."

"As it happens, she's invited me for Sunday dinner and I've accepted," Philip said.

Clark glanced up from his phone. "What about the tournament?"

"One dinner won't be the death of me," Philip said. "According to the schedule, the winner will be awarded the trophy at Balefire Beach on Monday afternoon."

"Yes," Florian said. "I originally planned to have it on Sunday, but Mother isn't exactly flexible when it comes to traditions."

"You don't have to tell me," Philip said. "I remember one year I suggested celebrating your father's birthday out of town and you should have seen the look of fury on your mother's face. She nearly hexed me right then and there."

"She always liked to celebrate birthdays at Thornhold," Linnea said.

"Thornhold?" Lewis perked up. "That's a hot spot too. Good place to find gold."

"Yes, it's where I live," Florian said.

Philip laughed. "I can just picture your mother's reaction to a lawn full of gamers."

"You haven't used Rose Cottage, have you?" I asked.

"No, you're safe back there," Florian said. "I didn't want to give the dog a stroke."

Or Marley. She was prone to anxiety and the last thing I needed was a parade of strange men outside our window or trampling her new herb garden.

Clark grimaced and tossed his phone onto the table. "Unlucky charms! I missed that vampire. Now he's going to come back stronger."

"Is that how it works?" I asked.

"Yes," Lewis said. "Any obstacle you don't defeat comes back stronger the next time. They feed off your failure."

"Sounds like Mother," Linnea said wryly.

"It's one of the aspects of the game I like," Philip said. "Keeps it challenging. Some of them get too repetitive. I get bored and stop playing."

"How are you already playing?" I asked. "Doesn't the tournament start at sunrise?"

"I'm playing the normal game right now for practice," Clark said. "The game will automatically switch to tournament mode when the time comes."

Marley snatched a warm roll from the bread plate. "Will you give us all your insider tips? My mom and I are going to join the tournament tomorrow."

"That's cool," Lewis said. "We don't see many mom and daughter duos at these events."

"I'm covering the tournament for the local paper," I said, "so Marley convinced me that I'd write a better story if I actually participated."

"That's not really how journalism works," Clark said, chewing his roll with his mouth open. "You're supposed to be an outside observer. It's called perspective."

I resisted the urge to give his bony leprechaun leg a swift kick under the table. "I know that, Clark, but it's not like it's a hard-hitting news item."

"It's a fluff piece," Clark said. "I get it."

I bristled. "I've written plenty of serious articles."

"This is Starry Hollow," Clark said. "I've seen your lighthouse restaurant and your aerial broomstick tour. I doubt it gets more serious here than which resident took home the blue ribbon for the annual homemade pie competition."

"And where are you from?" I asked. I didn't get the sense that Lewis and Clark were products of a paranormal gangster's paradise.

"We're from Charmed Corner," Lewis said.

I snorted. "Oh, yeah. That sounds like the criminal capital of the paranormal world right there," I said.

Marley seemed to sense my growing irritation because she plucked my phone from my handbag and opened the app. "It looks like we can add friends and keep track of each other's progress. What are your user names so I can add you?"

"An excellent suggestion," Philip said. "I'm wilywizard10."

"Cleverclover," Clark said.

"And I'm gardendelight," the gnome said. "What's yours?"

Marley's brow wrinkled as she looked at the screen. "Mom, I think you missed a letter on our name."

She showed me the phone and I began to choke on the roll I'd been chewing.

"What did you type?" Florian asked, grinning expectantly.

I grabbed the phone from Marley and stuffed it back into my handbag. "Never mind."

Florian fished the phone out of my handbag. "Oh, wow. That's unfortunate." He surveyed the table. "Anybody know how to edit a user name?"

"I don't think you can once you've created it," Clark said.

"What did you do?" Hudson asked. The teenager seemed to smell blood in the water.

I cleared my throat awkwardly. "I missed the letter 't' in thornybush," I said. "I wanted to do a play on our name-- Rose."

There was a momentary silence and then the snickers began in earnest.

My cheeks flamed. "The keypad is so tiny on the screen," I said. "I probably hit the backspace key by accident. My fingers always end up hitting the wrong spot."

"That never happens to me," Florian said.

Clark chuckled. "I can tell you'll be a real pro at this game. I'll be sure to wave to you from the winner's platform."

"We might be able to use a spell to fix it," Linnea said. "Let's try after dinner, okay?"

"I think you should leave it," Florian said. "With all the guys playing this weekend, you could end up with a string of suitors."

"I'm already spoken for, thank you," I said.

"Where is Alec tonight?" Linnea asked. She turned to address her guests. "Alec Hale is one of our more famous residents. He's the editor-in-chief of *Vox Populi*, the weekly paper, and he's a best-selling fantasy author."

"I remember Alec," Philip said. "A very solemn vampire, if I recall correctly."

"He has a great sense of humor once you get to know him," I said, probably a little defensively. "He's working on a book tonight, but he's coming by the cottage later. He was feeling inspired this week so he jumped down the rabbit hole and stayed there." My answer was partially true. The vampire also had a solo therapy appointment at dinnertime and I encouraged him not to cancel. It had taken too much effort to get him to commit to the appointment to let him bail for a family dinner. Couples counseling was all well and good, but the vampire had deep-seated issues that had nothing to do with me and everything to do with his early life.

"He should try to get one of his books adapted into a game," Florian said. "Wouldn't that be cool?"

"The only game I'm interested in right now is the one I plan to win," Clark said.

"Clark won the last WC tournament," Lewis said. "As the defending champion, he's feeling the pressure this weekend."

The leprechaun wrinkled his tiny nose. "I am not. I have every confidence I can get to the Emerald Chalice first."

"I'm sure everyone feels that way," I said. "Otherwise, they wouldn't bother participating."

Lewis smiled. "Not me. I know I won't win, but I love to try anyway. And it's fun to do stuff like this with Clark."

Clark's hand launched into the air in triumph, still

clutching his phone. "Got the bloodsucker!" He displayed the screenshot of his victory.

"Look, Mom. Your china cabinet is in the background," Bryn said.

"It's the augmented reality feature," Lewis said. "Makes it seem like the target is really in the same place as you."

"That's so cool," Marley said.

"I upload all my screenshots," Clark said. "I get a lot of followers on social media that way."

Lewis smirked. "And he likes to show off."

Clark went straight back to swiping on his phone. "I need to keep these digits limber for tomorrow's early start."

"Can I follow him on social media, Mom?" Marley asked.

"Nope. You know the rules." We'd already agreed that she was too young and that it was an unnecessary distraction.

Clark whooped again. "Uncovered a hidden nest of vamps."

Lewis leaned over to see his friend's screen. "Ooh, let me do that one."

"Congratulations," I said. "You definitely seem to have the hang of the game."

"You can tell me that again on Monday afternoon," Clark said. He set down his phone and wiggled his fingers. "Now, who's going to pass me the mashed potatoes?"

CHAPTER TWO

MARLEY and I left Palmetto House after dinner, trying to absorb the many tips we received from Philip and Lewis. Clark had disappeared after dessert for a solo practice session.

"If you and Alec want to go out tonight, I'm sure Mrs. Babcock can watch me," Marley said on the car ride home.

"What makes you think I want to go out tonight?" I asked.

"Florian mentioned an unofficial meetup at Balefire Beach," Marley said. "You should probably go and talk to players for your article. Make a date out of it."

"I don't need to go. I'm sure I'll get enough material this weekend to write the story," I said. I had to admit, though, the idea of going out was appealing. Recently, I'd been spending the bulk of my time in the triangle of work, motherhood, and Alec's current hermitic existence.

"I know you don't *need* to go, but it might be fun."

"Honestly, I think Alec will want to stay in," I said. "He had a long day." And I wanted to be available to talk to him about his therapy session if he felt so inclined. I tapped my fingernails on the steering wheel. "You know what? It's not terribly late. The three of us can play a game." Not Wizards Connect though. I knew a game like that wouldn't appeal to Alec.

Marley perked up. "Really? But we won't finish until past my bedtime."

"That's more of an issue for you than me," I said. Marley was the most routine-oriented child I knew.

She wore a big smile as she straightened in her seat. "Okay, maybe just an hour. I'll skip reading tonight."

While I knew other parents might cluck their tongues at a child skipping their bedtime reading, I knew Marley would come to no harm. Books were her favorite pastime and one evening of Scrabble wasn't going to ruin her.

Alec was waiting by his car outside the cottage when we arrived. As always, the sight of the tall, handsome vampire made my heart skip a beat.

He greeted me with a kiss on the lips. "I'm sorry I had to miss dinner. How did you find Philip?"

"He's pretty cool," Marley said. "I can see why Aunt Hyacinth isn't a fan though. He's way too laidback." She gave the vampire a hug. "We're going to play Scrabble. Hope you're up for the challenge."

She raced into the cottage to set up the game while I took PP3 out for a quick walk. Marley started yawning halfway into the game and decided to go to bed.

"We have a big weekend with the tournament and I have homework," she said. Her eyes were sleepy slits. "I should probably get a good night's sleep."

I kissed her on the top of the head. "We'll try not to disturb your beauty rest."

Marley hauled herself upstairs with the dog beside her.

I smiled at Alec. "Alone at last. I'll get more wine and the secret stash of cookies."

"You hide cookies from Marley?"

"I have to. If she gives me that sweet, innocent look, I'll hand over the whole tin and never get any." I hurried into the kitchen and grabbed the tin. When I returned, Alec had migrated to the sofa and stretched his long legs across the cushions. I set the tin on the coffee table and moved his legs to sit beneath them.

"How was your therapy session?"

"Fine," came the unenthusiastic reply.

"Did you actually talk or was it a staring contest?"

"It would be no contest, Ember. I'm a vampire." He paused for a beat. "There was a dialogue."

"That's good." I reached forward and opened the tin of cookies. They weren't my best effort, but they were…an effort.

His brow furrowed at the sight of them. "Chocolate chip?"

"Sort of. I ran out of chips because apparently I'd been snacking on the bag late at night and forgot they were for recipes."

He peered closer. "Then what are the other ingredients?"

"Whatever I had handy," I said.

He held one up to his mouth and hesitated. "The color is a little off."

"I ran out of milk so I may have substituted in Kahlua." I smiled. "I'd like to say it would be my first time getting drunk on cookies."

He grinned back at me. "I'm sure this is a story I need to hear."

"I was in high school. Mistakes were made." It was entirely possible that Marley had been conceived after indulging in a batch of Kahlua-based cookies.

"Do you think I might be one of them?" Alec casually bit into the cookie, as though he'd asked whether the sky was blue.

"What are you talking about?"

"This session with the therapist made me think."

"Good," I said. "That's the point. You need more introspection, but I wouldn't start jumping to crazy conclusions. That's my job."

Am I interrupting something? Raoul rounded the corner of the sofa.

You're always interrupting something. I noticed that he dragged a pizza box behind him. "Why are you bringing trash into the house?"

This isn't trash. It was a gift.

Another one? Why have you been the recipient of so many gifts lately? The other day he'd offered me a can of organic lentils. The can had been severely dented but still sealed.

Is it so strange that other animals like me? I'm adorable.

I examined the outside of the box. "This says it's Chicago-style deep dish. I thought you were partial to thin crust."

I'm partial to it, but I'm not going to look a gift pizza in the mouth. I'm going to put it IN my mouth. He tossed the box onto the coffee table and opened the lid, nearly knocking over the bottle of wine. *Anybody hungry?*

"That's kind of you," Alec said. Although he couldn't understand Raoul, the gesture was pretty obvious.

I stared at the metal object in the box. "Why is there a fork in the box?"

Raoul gave the fork a cursory glance. *How did that get in there? Must've slipped in at the dump.*

"Raoul, were you using a fork to eat pizza?" I tried not to sound too accusatory, but this was the raccoon that once said that eating pizza with a knife and fork was grounds for immediate deportation.

It's deep dish! I couldn't fold it in half or any of the things I'd normally do! He threw his paws in front of his face. *I've never been so ashamed.*

18

"Not even when you used the toilet bowl to brush your teeth?"

Not even then.

I turned toward Alec. "I can get you a plate if you're interested."

"No, thank you. Perhaps if there was something more exotic on offer like white cheese or pineapple."

The raccoon gaped at Alec, slack-jawed. *Pineapple on pizza is an abomination. How do you live an eternity and not know this?*

"Raoul, would you mind taking your pizza elsewhere? Alec and I are in the middle of a private discussion."

Is Bonkers around?

"I think she might be upstairs in Marley's room, but everyone's asleep." I snapped my fingers. "No pizza upstairs though. You can put it in the kitchen and invite Bonkers down to share it."

So uptight, he grumbled.

I glared at him. "What's that?"

I said I need to keep this box airtight. He slapped down the lid for good measure. *Don't want the pizza getting stale in the two minutes it takes me to run upstairs.*

The raccoon scrambled up the steps and I shifted my attention back to Alec. "Sorry about that. Now, what were you saying about your session? It got you thinking?"

"Nothing monumental," he said. "It's getting late and you mentioned an early start. Why don't we enjoy the wine?"

I didn't want to push the issue. I knew how Alec was. If he felt pressure, he'd withdraw and that was the opposite of what I wanted. I hoped he'd eventually feel comfortable enough to open up to me, but baby steps were okay.

"Where is the wine?"

"Oh, crap. I forgot." I'd been too excited about the secret cookies. "Red or white?"

He grinned. "Which do you think?"

"Red it is." I hurried into the kitchen, carrying the pizza box. While I uncorked a bottle and poured two glasses, Raoul and Bonkers entered the kitchen. "Is Marley asleep?"

Yeah, she left the light on again.

"That's okay. Whatever gets her to sleep on her own. You two stay in here and give us privacy, please."

My pleasure. The last thing I need is to see you two sucking face. I'll lose my appetite.

I returned to the sofa and handed Alec a glass. "Sorry. Everything takes longer with an audience."

He laughed softly. "I wouldn't know."

"We don't have to talk about therapy if you're not comfortable. Want to tell me about the book you're working on?"

"It's a story," he said. "With words."

"How illuminating." I curled up next to him. "Will you let me read the first draft?"

He kissed my forehead. "We'll cross that bridge when we come to it. I have no idea how long this one will take."

"I guess you don't have the same sense of urgency to finish a project when you're immortal," I said.

"It takes however long it takes," he said. "I prefer not to rush the story. I'd much rather it reveal itself to me."

"It's a book, not a ghost."

"All stories have ghosts," he said. "They're just not always apparent to the reader." He paused. "Or sometimes even the writer."

"You do sound very introspective tonight, Mr. Hale," I said. "I smell progress in the air."

"I suppose that's what therapy is meant to do," he said. He took a thoughtful sip of wine. "Speaking of progress, have you made any with Ivy?" As a descendant of the One True Witch and a High Priestess stripped of her title and her magic, Ivy Rose was one of my ancestors with a mysterious and unsavory story. My aunt had given Marley the wand that once belonged to Ivy, as well as the grimoire, and I'd discovered her Book of Shadows buried in the garden.

"I still haven't managed to open the Book of Shadows." The book was heavily warded and, despite my best efforts, I'd been unable to open it. "Apparently, there are archives in the coven's headquarters that might have information." Magnus Destry, the High Priest, had offered to snoop for me for reasons of his own.

"Excellent. Why haven't you gone to retrieve it? I would think you'd be breaking down the door."

"It's a restricted area and I'm not allowed in there," I said. "And no one's allowed to remove the contents." Although Alec was the height of discretion, it still seemed best not to mention Magnus's involvement.

"You don't wish to involve Hyacinth," Alec said.

I shook my head. "Not until I know more about Ivy."

"The event predates *Vox Populi* or I would check our records as well," Alec said.

"Thanks, I doubt the newspaper would have had the level of detail that the coven records will have though. I bet whatever happened doesn't exactly make the coven look good and that's why they hide the information."

"A familiar tale," Alec said.

"Is that why you withhold information?" I asked. I hadn't intended to ask the question, but the words came tumbling out before I could stop them.

"I beg your pardon?"

"Are you afraid that, if you share too much about yourself, it will somehow tarnish my opinion of you?" I snuggled closer. "Because I promise that won't happen. There's nothing you can say that will make me think less of you."

He rubbed my arm with affection. "That's kind of you to

say. I should probably let you get some rest before your early start." He leaned over and kissed me. "Sweet dreams."

"They'd be sweeter if you stayed."

"Another night this week, I promise." He kissed me again before rising to his feet. "Good luck with the tournament. Keep me informed."

I walked him to the door and kissed him again. It was always hard to watch him go. I enjoyed his company and wanted to make it last as long as possible, but he was right. I needed sleep. I was a monster without at least eight hours, which explained my mood most of the time.

It was only when I attempted to charge my phone at bedtime that I realized I didn't have it. I searched the cottage from top to bottom and even went out to the car to check under the seats. The last time I remembered having it was at Palmetto House. It was too late to bother Linnea now. I'd head over there first thing in the morning and grab it. If I timed my arrival right, maybe I'd be lucky and get breakfast while I was there. With the promise of bacon and buttermilk pancakes, I drifted into a peaceful slumber.

The next morning, I was up before sunrise, mostly because Marley had wandered in during the night and was now pushing me off the side of the bed. She blinked at me, bleary-eyed.

"How did you end up in here?" I asked.

"I had a bad dream about killing dragons," she said. "I like dragons. I want to make friends with them, not kill them."

I laughed. "I can see this tournament is going to go well for us."

"They should create a game that encourages collaboration," Marley said. "See how many successful coalitions you can build to achieve a set goal."

I flipped back the covers. "You start working on that one and we'll see how to make it happen."

"It's still early," Marley said. "You can go back to sleep."

"I left my phone at Linnea's," I said. "I need to head over and get it before the day gets away from me. Do you want to come?"

She stretched. "No, I'm going to try and sleep a little more."

"Why don't you try and sleep a little more in your own bed?"

"Fine." Marley rolled out of bed and stood with her shoulders hunched. "Don't let me sleep too late."

"I won't. We have a tournament to play, after all."

She blew a stray hair out of her eye. "That was my idea, wasn't it?"

"Yep." I quickly showered and dressed. My hair was still slightly damp when I slipped on shoes and headed for the car. I debated flying over, but I wasn't sure how easy it would be to land next to the inn. Her plot wasn't particularly big.

I parked right in front of the inn and ran up the steps to the front door. I knew it would be unlocked at this hour. Although it was early, the players would want to hit the ground running this morning.

There was no sign of anyone in the main living area. "Linnea," I called. No answer. I decided to check the kitchen. My stomach rumbled at the mere possibility of breakfast. I reached the doorway and came to an abrupt halt. "Linnea, are you okay?"

She kneeled on the floor, holding a cast iron skillet. It was only when I maneuvered around the island that I saw the problem. A leprechaun was face down on the floor in a puddle of blood. Linnea craned her neck to look at me, her eyes flooded with tears.

"It's Clark," she said. "He's dead."

CHAPTER THREE

DEPUTY BOLAN HUNCHED over the body. "See? This is what happens when leprechauns get treated like the redheaded stepchildren of the gaming world."

I peered at him. "You think Clark was killed because leprechauns are easy to kill in the game? A bit of a stretch, don't you think?"

The deputy straightened and crossed his arms. "Someone probably got caught up in nonsense of the game and decided to test the iron theory in real life."

"Are you really vulnerable to iron?" I asked. I began to fantasize about taking the deputy to the golf course for a 'friendly' game.

"If you bash me in the head with an iron skillet, I think you'll find I'm pretty vulnerable," he replied.

"It was my good skillet too," Linnea said. "The newer ones just aren't the same."

"Yes, it's the skillet we should be mourning," Deputy Bolan said.

"Have you seen Lewis?" I asked. "Someone will have to break the news about his friend."

"Unless he already knows," the deputy said ominously. "Who's the friend?"

"He's a gnome called Lewis," I said.

"Lewis and Clark?" the deputy queried. "Were they on some kind of gaming expedition together?"

"Marley will be pleased that someone else gets the reference," I said.

"I like human history," Deputy Bolan said. "Gives me a good giggle. It's really amusing when they think they've discovered places that had already been inhabited for thousands of years."

"Any idea where Lewis is?" I asked.

Linnea shook her head. "He missed breakfast this morning."

"Maybe the sheriff should check his room when he gets here," I said. Great popcorn balls of fire, the thought of a double homicide under Linnea's roof was nauseating.

The leprechaun hoisted up his belt. "I'll go," he said. "Which room?"

"Second door on the right," Linnea said.

"If you're not back in ten minutes, we'll presume the worst," I called after him. He didn't bother to turn around, not even to scowl.

Linnea's hand covered her mouth as she stared at the lifeless body. "How could something like this happen under my own roof?"

"It only takes a split second to whack someone with a skillet," I said. "They probably ran straight out the back door with no one the wiser."

"This is going to be terrible for business," Linnea said. "Word is going to get around that Palmetto House is Starry Hollow's murder capital."

I slung an arm across her shoulders. "And if that happens,

you can just turn the inn into its own attraction. Tourists love murdery places."

"Toss in a few ghosts and you'll be golden." Sheriff Granger Nash swaggered into the kitchen. "You could have your own Casper's Revenge-type place." Casper's Revenge was a local inn managed entirely by ghosts. He stopped short at the sight of the dead leprechaun. "I guess this is our potential ghost."

"Clark," I said. "He was in town for the tournament."

"At first glance I thought he was Bolan." Sheriff Nash rubbed his forehead. "I gotta admit my heart skipped a beat."

"Are you saying all leprechauns look alike?" I clucked my tongue. "Don't let the deputy here you say that."

"I said at first glance," he said. "To be fair, they're both small and green."

"And mouthy," I said. "Clark wasn't exactly a shrinking clover."

The sheriff surveyed the kitchen. "Where is my mouthy little green guy?"

"Upstairs," I said. "Checking for Clark's friend, Lewis."

He started. "You mean we might have two victims?"

"Only one, thank the gods," Deputy Bolan's voice rang out.

The tightening in my chest released. One victim was bad enough, but two would have been a lot worse. Starry Hollow would have been wiped off the map for any future events.

The living leprechaun reappeared in the kitchen. "There's no corpse. His stuff is still there, but he's not."

"He's probably already out gaming," I said. "This tournament is no joke to them."

"Which is probably why we're looking at a murder victim," the sheriff said. He seemed to notice my outfit for the first time. "You're here bright and early, Rose. Did you sleep here?"

"No, I left my phone here at dinner," I said.

Linnea smacked her forehead. "Yes, I found it and put it in my purse." She motioned to the back of the kitchen door. "It's on the hook."

I crossed the kitchen and rooted around in her bag until I found my phone. "Thanks."

Linnea wore a pained expression. "Do you really think someone killed Clark over a stupid game?"

"The game isn't stupid to them," I said. "I noticed Clark doing hand exercises at dinner, limbering up for the weekend."

"Did Clark travel here with anyone aside from Lewis?" the sheriff asked.

"No," Linnea said. "They're friends from home and they came together. That's it."

"Anyone else staying here aside from you and the kids?" the sheriff asked.

"My cousin, Philip Muldoon," Linnea said.

The sheriff raised his eyebrows. "A Muldoon, huh? Why not stay at Thornhold?"

"He and Aunt Hyacinth aren't exactly best buds," I said.

His mouth twitched. "I like the guy already."

"Philip went out right before breakfast," Linnea said.

"Did he have any interaction with the victim?" the sheriff asked.

"No, they missed each other by a hair. Philip said he had to defeat two werewolves, a vampire, and a dragon before lunch, so there was no time to waste."

"I don't know how you can slaughter that many creatures on an empty stomach," Deputy Bolan said.

"He took a banana and a bottle of water," Linnea said. "Let me try calling him now." She clicked the phone and held it to her ear. "Straight to voicemail."

Deputy Bolan whipped out his roll of tape to secure the

scene. "This town could be flooded with suspects. How are we going to track them all down?"

"Just find the hot spots," I said. "Florian can tell you where they are."

Sheriff Nash gave me his full attention. "Hot spots?"

"He knows where you can battle a dragon," I said. "That sort of thing. It will make it easier to find Philip and anybody else you want to question."

Deputy Bolan crouched down to examine the victim. "His phone is missing."

"Could he have left it in his room?" the sheriff asked.

Linnea shook her head. "He had it when I saw him at breakfast. As far as I know, he never left this floor. I went back downstairs to shower."

"Clark didn't seem the type to ever be separated from his phone," I said. I pictured him cuddling the device in bed at night.

Linnea glanced at her own phone. "I texted Florian. He said that Philip is an experienced player, so he could be anywhere from werewolves to vampires to dragons."

"Where are those hot spots?" the sheriff asked.

Linnea scanned the text. "He said the two most likely places now are Balefire Beach and Haverford House."

"I can check Haverford House," I said. It would be good to let Artemis know that her property would be inundated with paranormals this weekend, if Florian hadn't already warned her. The elderly witch might barricade herself inside the house, not that she was prone to leave.

The sheriff looked at me. "You don't need to feel obligated to help."

I put my hands on my hips. "Since when will I voluntarily sit out of an investigation?"

"Florian asks that you please not report this as part of your article on the tournament, Ember," Linnea said.

"We need to find out what happened first," I said. "We don't know that his death is related to the tournament."

"The iron weapon says otherwise," the deputy said, "but I'm willing to reserve judgment."

"You're just salty because the victim is a leprechaun," I said. "His death isn't a reflection on your species, you know. We'd all succumb to a cast iron skillet."

"Don't mind him. He was born salty," the sheriff said.

The deputy shot me an aggrieved look. "I'll check out the beach. It's on my way home anyway and I need to grab my lunch. I forgot it earlier. My husband will kill me if he sees it there when he comes home. He made it special."

Sheriff Nash cast me a sidelong glance. "Mind if I join you at Haverford House?"

I suddenly felt awkward having volunteered to go there. I didn't want the sheriff to feel uncomfortable during his own investigation. "I can skip it. I'm sure there are other ways I can help."

"Don't back out on me now, Rose," the sheriff said. "I'm sure Artemis will be pleased to see you."

"If you're sure," I said.

"You two head over there. I'll take care of things here before I go to the beach," Deputy Bolan said.

The sheriff faced me. "How about I drive?"

I squinted. "Why do I get the sense that you're placing judgment on my driving skills?"

"Because I've seen you behind the wheel enough times to know." He paused. "And your taste in music is questionable."

My jaw unhinged. "I know you're not making disparaging remarks about Billy Joel and Bruce Springsteen."

He chuckled as he headed toward the front door. I hurried after him, still defending myself.

"Relax, Rose," he said, unlocking the car doors. "I'll treat your ears to actual music. Consider it a gift."

I slid into the passenger seat and buckled my seatbelt. "I know what good music sounds like, thank you. I'm from New Jersey."

"Exactly," the sheriff said. The engine roared to life and away we went. Once we were safely on the road, he turned up the volume on the current song.

I started to laugh. "You can't be serious. This is a joke, right?" Even my father would've laughed at Bobby Darin's *Dream Lover*.

He shot me a quick glance. "What? This song is great."

"If you're a World War II veteran, sure," I said. "If you're going old school, you should at least try Elvis or Frank Sinatra." I leaned over. "Sinatra is from New Jersey, you know."

"Duly noted."

"I didn't realize you listened to any music from the human world."

"I didn't always," he said. "I started listening to find something good after…" He trailed off.

"After what?"

"After you came to town and played all these songs I hadn't heard before." He seemed slightly embarrassed. "And I did karaoke that one night, remember?"

"How could I forget? You and Alec both…" I stopped abruptly. It seemed too close for comfort to reminisce about a competition between them.

"We're here." The sheriff pulled into the driveway at Haverford House.

I spotted several gamers roaming the grounds. No Philip or Lewis though. "Let me send a quick text to Marley and make sure she's awake and dressed." She replied with an eye roll emoji. Typical tween.

I knocked and wasn't at all surprised when an unseen hand pulled open the door. I entered first with the sheriff close enough behind me that I could feel his breath on my neck. I turned to look at him.

"Have you forgotten the notion of personal space?" I wondered if he was anxious about Jefferson, the ghostly manservant that took care of Artemis in more ways than I cared to think about.

"What makes you say that?" he asked. He practically bumped into me on the way to the parlor.

"No reason," I said. I bit the inside of my cheek to keep from laughing. My brow lifted as we entered the parlor. It was standing room only and Artemis sat in her chair, lording over all of the visitors. China teacups were everywhere I looked.

"Phones go in the basket," a troll said. His chubby finger pointed to the floating wicker basket filled with phones.

"The sheriff and I will keep our phones," I said. "Thank you, Jefferson."

Artemis smiled at us. "What a pleasant surprise. I've had so many unexpected guests this weekend. It's been splendid."

So much for Florian letting the elderly witch know to expect trespassers. At least she took it in stride. I'd have reached for my wand if I'd spotted groups of paranormals swarming the land outside Rose Cottage. Of course, that wasn't necessarily threatening. With my luck, I'd accidentally use a Big Bad Wolf spell and they'd spend the next hour trying to knock down my house while I raged about the hair I forgot to tweeze on my chinny chin chin.

Artemis addressed the gamers. "Everyone, these are my friends, Ember Rose and Sheriff Nash."

"Cool," a young elf said. He didn't look older than sixteen. "You're a real sheriff?"

The werewolf tapped his badge. "The star doesn't lie."

I stifled a laugh.

"What's that, Rose? Got a frog in your throat?"

31

I cleared my throat. "No, nothing. Sorry."

"We're looking for a wizard named Philip Muldoon and a gnome called Lewis," the sheriff said. "Has anyone seen them?"

"I saw Lewis out back about twenty minutes ago," the troll said. "He was trying to battle a dragon."

"I gave up," the elf said. "The dragon kept winning and I ran out of gold to buy more weapons."

"Tea and biscuits are welcome alternatives to dragon killing, aren't they, boys?" Artemis asked pleasantly. She reminded me of Wendy from Peter Pan, appeasing the Lost Boys.

Murmurs of asset followed her statement.

"Artemis is going to show me how to embroider a dragon," another player said. "I want to hang it on my bedroom wall at home."

I started to wonder if Artemis had bewitched these boys.

"If anyone sees Lewis or Philip, would you ask them to contact the sheriff's office?" Sheriff Nash asked.

"Their user names are gardendelight and wilywizard10," I added.

Sheriff Nash cut me a quick glance. "That's actually useful information, Rose."

I shrugged. "It's been known to happen."

"Artemis, do you mind if we walk the property to see if either of these gentlemen is roaming around?" the sheriff asked.

"By all means," she said. "It's practically a party out there. Tell anyone you see that I have plenty of tea and biscuits."

"Her milkshake brings all the boys to the yard," I whispered as we left the house.

"Her milkshake is about two hundred years old," the sheriff said. "I think it's probably curdled by now."

We walked the length of the property and checked the

woods behind the house. We crossed paths with plenty of players but no one had seen Philip or Lewis.

"I'll check with Bolan and see if he's had better luck," the sheriff said.

"Would you mind dropping me back at my car? I want to pick up Marley since I promised her that we could play the game today."

"No problem."

I also wanted to be able to keep my ears open for information. If there was a player in town cold-blooded enough to kill more than the paranormals in the game, then we were all at risk.

CHAPTER FOUR

I PICKED up an eager Marley and we headed back to Palmetto House so that I could check on Linnea. Marley happily ran to the backyard to play with the other gamers.

"Any sign of Philip?" I asked. Linnea and Aster were in the kitchen, baking a pie for dessert this evening. I inhaled the scent of cinnamon and cloves.

"Not yet," Linnea said. "He's not answering his phone either, but that's not a surprise. According to some of the players I've met today, they turn notifications off during the tournament so an incoming text or call can't screw them up."

I surveyed the kitchen floor. "Good job cleaning. You can't even tell there was a murder committed here earlier today."

Linnea scowled. "I had to wait for the green light. Deputy Bolan was methodical. I swear he even checked in the nooks and crannies of the nooks and crannies."

"Well, I would think that's what you'd want from the deputy investigating your murder," Aster said. She dusted the flour from her hands and placed them on her hips. "Now, can we talk about performing a cleansing spell on the house?"

I frowned. "I thought you just said you cleaned already."

"I'm not talking about the blood," Aster said. "I'm talking about expelling the negative energy. You don't want any lingering malevolence as a result of the murder. That's a recipe for an angry ghost."

Linnea heaved a sigh. "Like I don't have enough to do as it is. I still have guests and players meandering around my yard."

Aster moved to the cupboard and began pulling out jars of herbs. "Come on. It won't take long. Who knows? Maybe it will even help speed along the investigation."

My eyes widened. "The cleansing spell can do that?" In that case, why didn't the sheriff keep a witch or wizard on his payroll?

Aster shrugged. "Not really, but wouldn't it be nice?" She set the jars on the counter. "We need to close all the doors and windows before we start."

My gaze swept the kitchen. "Wouldn't it make sense to keep them open? Doesn't the negative energy need somewhere to go?"

"That's not how it works," Linnea said. "Have you not done one of these before?" She quickly shook her head. "Of course not. Why would you have? Well, Mother will be pleased. She'll consider this a learning opportunity for you."

"Does that mean I can skip one of my lessons this week?" I asked hopefully. Thanks to a change in the lineup, Marigold and Hazel were both scheduled for Monday.

"I sincerely doubt it," Aster said. "You know how committed Mother is to making sure you're a witch of the highest caliber."

"You know what they say," I said. "Shoot for the stars and disappoint everyone." I crossed the room to close the window over the kitchen sink. "What else do we need to do?"

"You two prepare the spell and I'll go close the other

windows," Linnea said. "I know the one in Hudson's bedroom is open because I had to air out the smell of stinky gym socks." As an athletic teenager, Hudson hadn't yet mastered the lost art of cleaning up after himself. "Further proof that he is his father's son." Linnea headed downstairs to the family living quarters.

"I need a bucket of water," Aster said.

I located a small bucket under the sink and started to fill it. "I hope your cousin is okay."

"I'm sure he's fine," Aster said. "Cousin Philip is like a tumbleweed. He just trundles along haphazardly without a care in the world. It's one of the qualities that Mother despises about him."

I snorted. "It seems an odd thing to despise. I can understand if he leaves nail clippings on the kitchen counter or puts the toilet paper roll on the wrong way, but why is living his best life a problem?"

"His behavior simply doesn't fit her view of what a Muldoon should be," Aster said. "I was much younger at the time, of course, but I remember having a very clear sense of how she felt about him."

"She doesn't exactly have a poker face," I said. More like a you'll-wish-you'd-been-smacked-with-a-cast-iron-skillet face. "It's a shame that Philip hasn't been back since your father's funeral. Even though your mother doesn't like him, it sounds like the three of you might have missed out on a good relationship with him." I knew what that was like. My own father had spirited me away after my mother's death and took me to live in the human world, away from the influence of Aunt Hyacinth. I grew up in Maple Shade, New Jersey, not knowing that I was descended from a long line of esteemed witches and wizards. As direct descendants of the One True Witch, members of the Rose family were like minor celebrities in Starry Hollow simply because of our DNA.

"I'm glad Philip decided to come for the tournament," Aster said. "At least it gave him an excuse to see us." She joined me at the sink and placed a squat candle in the bucket to float on the surface of the water. Then she tipped in the mixture of herbs.

"Windows are done," Linnea said, returning to the kitchen.

Aster pulled out her wand and aimed it at the candle. "*Incendo*." A flame flickered and Aster scooped up the bucket. "We need to stand in the middle of each room and place the bucket between us. She turned and put the bucket on the floor of the kitchen. "We should start here since this room is the most affected."

She wiggled her fingers, so Linnea and I stood on either side of her and joined hands.

"Close your eyes and imagine that all the negative energy is being drawn to the fire," Linnea said.

"Do we chant?" I asked. It seemed like a safe assumption.

"Yes, *emigro, evanesco*," Aster said. "You'll feel the shift in the air when the room has been cleansed. Then we'll move on to the next room. We need to do the whole house because we don't know which rooms might be impacted."

We'd only managed two rounds of chants when there was a knock at the kitchen door. Linnea groaned in exasperation and opened the door. An elf stood on the step, hopping from foot to foot.

"The bathroom is around the corner," Linnea said, pointing. The elf rushed forward and Linnea poked her head outside. "If anyone else needs the bathroom, do it now! We can't have these interruptions or the ritual will be ruined!"

No one else came forward and Linnea slammed the door behind the retreating elf. I texted Marley to wait outside until I said otherwise.

We completed the ritual in the kitchen without interruption this time. I felt the shift, just the way Linnea had described it.

"Can all witches do this?" I asked.

"I would think so," Aster said. "Why?"

"I don't always know which abilities are special, like One True Witch genes at work, and which ones are routine coven magic."

"The more magic you perform, the more you'll learn the difference," Aster said.

I suppressed a smile. "Now you sound like Aunt Hyacinth."

"It's true though," Aster said. "Eventually, you'll develop an innate sense of what's 'normal witch' and what's 'super-power witch.'"

"Did you ever perform magic so powerful that you worried you'd lose control?" I asked.

Aster and Linnea exchanged looks. "Is this about Ivy again?" Linnea asked.

I lowered my gaze to stare into the bucket. "Maybe."

"I'd worry more about mastering the basics and less about burning down the town," Aster said.

I reeled back. "Did Ivy burn down the town?"

Aster clutched her pearls. "Goddess no, it was just an extreme example," she said.

"Let's do Clark's room next," Linnea said.

"Good idea," Aster said.

As we went to each room of the house, I understood why Linnea was annoyed with having to perform the spell. The house cleanse was incredibly time-consuming. I felt uneasy in Clark's room, as though icy fingers were trailing down my spine. Even though I was sure it was all in my head, it made me chant faster and with more enthusiasm in the hopes that any residual energy would dissipate quickly. Once we finished the final room, we carried the bucket to the front door and extinguished the flame. Linnea took the bucket down the front steps and walked to the edge of her property line, where she poured the contents on the ground.

"We need to open a window now," Aster said.

"I'll go back to the kitchen and open the one over the sink," I offered. As I pushed up the pane, I spotted Philip coming up the back steps. The kitchen door opened and the wizard snapped back at the sight of me.

"Sorry about that," he said, breaking into nervous laughter. "I wasn't expecting to see anyone so close to the door." He held up his phone. "It probably doesn't help that I have my nose buried in this."

"How's it going?" I asked.

He crossed the threshold into the kitchen and closed the door behind him. "Not too bad. I managed to pick up extra gold after lunch, so that was a boon." He sniffed the air. "The pie smells delicious."

Linnea and Aster appeared in the doorway at the sound of Philip's voice.

"Thank the gods," Linnea said. "Where have you been? We've been worried about you."

Philip's brow furrowed. "What's the problem? I've been busy with the tournament all day."

"Do you know about Clark?" I asked.

Philip scratched his head. "What about him? Did he win already?" He made a dismissive noise. "No, that's not possible. No one could have reached the Emerald Chalice yet."

"Philip," Linnea said gently. "Clark is dead. Someone murdered him this morning."

Philip seemed to slowly digest the news. "Where?"

Aster pointed. "Exactly where you're standing now."

Philip instinctively jumped backward as though the leprechaun's body was still there. "Someone killed Clark in your kitchen?"

"Believe me, I'm about as thrilled as you would expect," Linnea said. "The killer used my good cast iron skillet."

"Who would do such a thing?" Philip asked.

"I know," Linnea said. "They could have at least had the decency to use their own pan."

"Has the murderer been caught?" Philip asked.

"No," I said. "The sheriff and deputy are investigating. We looked for you earlier at Haverford House. We thought you might be battling the dragon there."

Philip expelled a breath. "I was, but it took me longer to get there than I expected. My battle with the magic eel delayed me."

"There's a magic eel?" I asked. "Is that a real thing?"

"It's a secret challenge you can unlock for extra gold," Philip said. "Clark's actually the one who told me about it. He discovered it last night during his practice session and showed me the screenshot."

"It's like the nerd version of a selfie," I said.

"After that I ran out of supplies and had to go and do an extra challenge to replenish." He paused. "That's all gibberish to you, isn't it?"

"We need to let the sheriff know that you're here," I said. "He'll want to speak to you."

Philip continued to glance at his phone, seemingly unable to stop playing the game during this important conversation. "I'm not sure how much help I can be. I don't know anything. I haven't even seen him since last night."

"How late?" I asked.

"Maybe midnight. We were both in the backyard completing extra challenges to stock up on gold and supplies for this morning."

"Was it just the two of you?" I asked.

He swiped on his phone. "No, Lewis was there and a few other players came by."

"Did anything unusual happen?" I asked. "Any arguments that involved Clark?"

Philip considered the question. "As a matter of fact, yes. A werebear by the name of Buck was giving Clark a hard time."

"About what?" I asked.

"Clark took a box of flamethrowers after they raided a vampire's nest together," Philip said.

"I assume we're talking about the game," I said.

"That's right. Sometimes you can complete challenges as a team when they're particularly difficult. During that time, certain items become the community property of the group and some of the more unscrupulous players will walk off with items they didn't own at the beginning of the challenge," Philip explained.

"I imagine Buck was unhappy about this," I said.

Philip nodded. "I ended up having to use magic to calm them down. Trust me when I tell you that doesn't happen very often."

"Cousin Philip doesn't tend to use magic," Linnea said. "He's more of a non-practicing wizard."

"Not so much non-practicing as not-so-eagerly practicing," Philip said. "I spend a lot of time in the human world, so I find it makes sense to limit how often I use magic."

I imagined that was something else Aunt Hyacinth didn't like about him. She took great pride in the powers of the Rose-Muldoon family and was probably personally offended that someone with inherent talent like Philip's would choose to ignore it.

"Any chance you know where we can find Buck?" I asked.

Philip tapped on his phone screen. "I passed him about an hour ago. He was headed due east away from the beach."

"Can you describe him?" I asked.

Philip wore a vague smile. "He's about what you'd expect a werebear to look like."

"The huggable kind or the grizzly kind?" I asked.

Philip rubbed his chin. "A mixture, I'd say. He's wearing a Chicago Bears T-shirt, if that helps."

"Can I get you something to eat or drink, Philip?" Linnea asked.

"I just came in for a quick snack and a bathroom break," Philip said. "Then I'm heading straight back out. From what I hear, there are only a handful of players ahead of me. I still have a shot at winning."

"I'd make myself available to the sheriff if I were you," I said. "He'd like nothing better than to annoy Aunt Hyacinth by locking up one of her relatives and making her come down to the office to bail you out."

Philip chuckled. "I think she'd rather let me rot, but I promise I'll reach out and let him know where he can find me. I have an ogre to defeat next."

"Cousin Philip, I'm surprised," Linnea said. "I don't recall you being so competitive."

Philip gave us a sheepish grin. "I'm not really. Occasionally, I'll get caught up in the spirit of the game. When you realize winning is actually a possibility, you tend to feel a little more compelled to achieve, although we still have tomorrow to get through."

It seemed to me that nothing about what happened today was in the spirit of the game. A player was down and everyone carried on like it was business as usual. When you spent most hours of the day killing paranormals on a screen, an actual death probably did seem like business as usual. The fact that Clark was killed by iron didn't help either.

"Good luck with the rest of the tournament," I said. "I guess I'll see you at dinner tomorrow at Thornhold."

"I look forward to it," Philip said.

My gaze drifted to the floor where Clark's body had been. Too bad for the leprechaun it was game over.

CHAPTER FIVE

SHERIFF NASH WAS busy questioning a couple of players who'd been spotted with Clark on Friday afternoon before the tournament officially started, so Deputy Bolan and I were given the task of tracking down Buck. We found the werebear wandering the pavement not far from the Black Cloak Academy. With his broad physique and T-shirt with the Chicago Bears logo, he was easy to spot. He appeared a little lost, staring at his phone and then glancing around at his surroundings. Deputy Bolan pulled the car alongside the curb and rolled down the window.

"Are you Buck?" the deputy asked.

"Yeah, that's me." The werebear barely glanced up from his phone. "Can you tell me where the ash tree is? According to the game, it should be right around here." He looked over each shoulder. "I don't see any big ash tree though." He chuckled to himself. "Big ash tree. Like ass. Get it?"

"How many hours straight have you been playing this game?" I asked. To be fair, he wasn't alone. Wyatt would have appreciated the joke.

"Not long enough to win, apparently," Buck said. "I deftnitely think it's going to take someone until late tomorrow afternoon. This tournament is harder than the last one."

"I think you're looking for the Tree of Bounty," Deputy Bolan said. "I know where it is. Why don't you get in the back and I'll drive you there?"

Buck seemed pleased with this development. "That's what I call service." He slid into the backseat and closed the door. "The last time I was in the back of a cop car was under much less pleasant circumstances."

Well, that was an interesting tidbit. I craned my neck to look at him. "Drunk and disorderly?"

"No…" He stopped to think. "Actually, yes. I was so drunk I forgot I was drunk." He slapped his knee. "I ended up with two black eyes, but you should've seen Sheila."

My eyes popped. "Sheila?"

"Relax, she's a Yeti. She usually kicks my ash." He laughed again at his joke.

"What did you do to deserve two black eyes?" I asked.

"I accidentally drank her bottle of Moscato."

I frowned. "How do you accidentally drink someone's bottle of wine?"

He shrugged. "I thought it was sparkling water. I chugged it so fast that I didn't notice her freaking out until she was pummeling me."

"Hence the drunk and disorderly," I said.

Buck peered out the window. "Am I really that far away from the tree that we need to drive? I thought this town was walkable. That was part of the reason for hosting the tournament here."

Deputy Bolan locked the doors. "I thought the drive would give us the chance to talk in private. You don't want any of your buddies to hear that you're being interrogated about a murder."

Buck laughed under his breath. "Is this part of the game? Because I didn't pay extra for bonus content."

"It's not part of the game," Deputy Bolan said. His gaze flicked to the rearview mirror. "Tell us what happened between you and Clark last night."

"Who's Clark?" Buck asked.

I craned my neck to look at him. "Little green guy that you argued with at Palmetto House last night."

"Hey," Deputy Bolan objected. "Easy on the little and green."

I flashed him an innocent look. "What? It's an accurate description."

"What the hell?" Buck said. "Is that little thief going around telling people I killed someone? What's his problem?"

I twisted further to look at him. "No, that little thief is the one who's been murdered."

The color drained from Buck's round face. "He's dead?"

"His body was found this morning in the kitchen of Palmetto House," I said. "You knew he was staying there because that's where you argued with him last night."

Buck began typing quickly on his phone.

"What are you doing?" I asked.

Buck didn't bother to glance up at me. "Letting my friends know that the chalice is still up for grabs." He typed so quickly that it was hard to imagine he could form words. "Do you happen to have his phone?"

Deputy Bolan eyed him closely. "No, why do you ask?"

"If he's dead, I can use his phone to take back my stuff that he stole. And I'll take a few of his things for good measure. Payback."

"We don't have his phone." I shifted my gaze to Deputy Bolan, unwilling to let Buck see how horrified I was by his insensitivity.

Deputy Bolan turned down a dirt path. "Can you tell us where you were this morning?"

"All over town," he replied. "Playing in a tournament, remember?" He waved his phone at the rearview mirror.

"How about you be more specific?" Deputy Bolan asked. His tight expression told me that he'd had enough of Buck the werebear.

Buck scowled. "Are you seriously questioning me about this little dude's death? No way would I risk losing a tournament by killing someone. That's just nuts."

"It's also nuts to be focused on taking the belongings of a dead player rather than acknowledging what happened to him," I said.

Buck set the phone on his thigh and looked at me. "I'm sorry he's dead, okay? But I didn't have anything to do with it, so I don't see why it should interrupt the tournament. I still have a chance to win and I'm not going to let anything get in my way." He glanced out the window. "Hey, is that the tree?"

I followed his gaze to see an enormous tree towering over the others in the woods.

"This tree has historic significance in Starry Hollow," Deputy Bolan said. "That's probably why it's part of the game."

"No wonder people are having a hard time completing this challenge," Buck said. "This tree is hard to find."

"That's probably by design," the deputy said. "Makes it a little more challenging."

Buck tried to open the door but found it was locked. "Deputy Dude, can you let me out so I can complete this challenge?"

"When we're finished talking, I'd be happy to," the leprechaun said.

A sheen of sweat appeared on Buck's forehead when he

noticed a couple of players coming up the path behind us. "Can we hurry it up? I need to finish the challenge before these guys do. If they take the magic beans, then I have to wait for them to regrow before I can do it. It'll slow me down."

"That's a shame," the deputy said, in a way that suggested it was most definitely not. "Want to run through your morning with us?"

Buck slumped against the back of the seat, visibly defeated. "I got up around six and ate a bagel at the coffee shop."

"Which one?" I asked.

"Poppy seed," he said.

I closed my eyes and mentally counted to ten. "Which coffee shop, not which bagel?"

"Oh, right. Caffeinated Cauldron," he said. "And I had a cup of peppermint tea."

"No coffee for your long day?" I asked.

He cringed. "No way. Coffee does a number on my stomach and I can't afford to spend half the day in the bathroom."

"Were you by yourself?" the deputy asked.

"Yeah, but you can ask the barista. She was asking me lots of questions about the game, so I think she'll remember me."

"What time did you leave there?" I asked.

He began scrolling through his phone. "About six forty-five. Then I went to battle some werewolves."

"How can you be so sure of the time?" I asked.

He waved the phone. "The game tells me what time I completed challenges and battles. I killed the first werewolf at six forty-eight, but the other one took longer. I didn't finish until twelve past seven."

The deputy turned and held out his hand. "I think I'm going to need to take a look at your phone."

Buck clutched the device against his chest. "No way. Not today. You can have it after the competition finishes tomorrow but not before."

"Buck, a very serious crime has been committed during this tournament," I said. "Would you rather be arrested for murder and spend the rest of the tournament in a jail cell or would you rather cooperate now for a few minutes and be able to keep playing?"

Buck muttered a string of obscenities as he handed over the phone. "Can you scroll quickly? I've seen these guys play and they're slow. I'm pretty sure if there's not too much of a gap, I can overtake them."

I watched Deputy Bolan's expression as he flicked through the information on Buck's phone. He paused on one of the pages.

"Okay, Buck. You're free to go for now. But I'm going to tell you not to leave town until this investigation is finished." He fixed the werebear with a hard stare. "You got that?"

"Got it." He fumbled with the door handle. "Can you let me out now?"

The deputy unlocked the door and Buck bolted from the backseat, slamming the door behind him. I looked at the deputy. "He's not our guy, is he?"

"I wouldn't have let him out if he was. All of his movements this morning are right there on the phone. The closest he came to Palmetto House was the coffee shop."

"Look on the bright side," I said. "All the gamers should have the same type of alibi. Something like this should make the investigation easier."

"Let's hope. The last thing I want is for the town to be overrun with gamers for another week."

"We should talk to some of these players," I said, nodding toward the guys near the tree. "See if anyone's heard anything."

Deputy Bolan glowered. "The only thing these guys have likely heard is the sound of their phone batteries dying."

The moment I left the car, a wave of emotions overwhelmed me and I staggered back a few steps until I regained my composure.

"You okay, Rose?" Deputy Bolan asked.

I blinked and looked around. "You don't feel that?"

He held his palm open as though testing for raindrops. "No."

There was a weight to the air that I couldn't quite describe. Not humidity but something else. Darkness. I pushed past the sensation as we approached a trio of werewolves. Their heads were bent together and they were swearing at their phones with equal enthusiasm.

"Excuse me," I said.

The middle head jerked up to look at me. "Not now, lady. I'm battling a fanger."

"Only because you couldn't kill one of us in real life," someone said.

I turned to see a vampire with a phone in his hand, lingering close to the ash tree and even closer to his pixie companion. She seemed unable to take her eyes off him. Getting a little nerd action during the tournament. Good for them.

"Personally, I like killing the centaurs," the vampire said. "I loathe those guys."

"We're looking for a gnome named Lewis," I said. "Has anyone seen him?"

No one answered. They were too busy defeating their foes.

"Does anyone here know Clark?" I asked. "He's a leprechaun about…" I grabbed Deputy Bolan and placed him in front of me. "This tall. Similar grumpy attitude."

The deputy wrenched himself free and shot me a menacing look.

"I remember that guy," the middle werewolf said. "Didn't he win the last tournament?"

"That's him," I said. "Clark."

I noticed the middle werewolf nudge the one to his left and they began arguing in heated whispers.

"Gentlemen, don't be afraid to share with the class," I said.

"Bigsby has something to tell you," the middle werewolf said.

The werewolf on the left wore a guilty expression. His hand slid into his jacket pocket and produced a phone. "I think this might belong to Clark. I was going to find him and give it back, I swear."

"I'll take that." The deputy took out a glove and put it on before snatching the phone.

"Dude, I don't have cooties," the werewolf said.

The deputy studied the screen. "What makes you think it belongs to Clark?"

"I remember his user name from the last tournament," Bigsby said. "Cleverclover."

My heart jolted. "That's his." I leaned over Deputy Bolan's shoulder for a better view of the phone.

"Why didn't you try to find him straight away and give it back?" the deputy asked.

"Because he won last time," Bigsby said. "I figured the longer I kept hold of it, the less likely he'd be able to catch up."

"Well, there's no chance of him winning this time," the deputy said. "Clark is dead."

"All his gold is missing," I said.

"It was like that when I found it," Bigsby said. He lowered his head. "I checked because I was going to take his supplies, but they were already gone."

I squinted at the screen. "Is there a way to see who took it?"

Bigsby moved closer. "Can I touch it?"

"Go ahead," the deputy said. "Your fingerprints are already all over it."

Bigsby clicked an icon in the corner. "User name is obiwandkenobi."

The vampire by the tree snorted. "Ridiculous."

"What's your name then?" I asked.

"Vladtheinhaler," he said. "If you must know, I suffer from asthma." He pulled out his inhaler and shook it.

"Loser," one of the werewolves said with an exaggerated cough.

"I think it's sexy," the pixie proclaimed.

Okay, I wouldn't go that far. Someone was clearly smitten.

"How can a vampire have asthma?" I asked. "They don't even breathe."

"My mother was human," vladtheinhaler said. "Which is why I'm a watered-down version of my father."

"You have fangs and an attitude," I said. "Seems vampiric enough to me."

"I don't have preternatural speed or strength. I can't read minds. The woman robbed me of all the best vampire parts."

The pixie batted her lashes. "Not *all* the best parts."

I wondered if Marley would say that about her father one day—that Karl robbed her of her full magical strength. Somehow, I doubted it.

"Anybody know obiwandkenobi?" the deputy asked.

They shook their heads.

"Where did you find the phone?" Deputy Bolan asked.

"In the bushes over there," Bigsby said. He pointed to wild burstberry bushes near the ash tree. "I went to take a leak and I saw it when the sunlight hit the screen. It was still on."

"How long ago was that?" I asked.

"Maybe an hour?" Bigsby looked at his friends for confirmation.

I pressed my hand to my forehead. "I knew his user name. I could have looked to see his progress."

"It's nice like you expected him to have any. He's dead." Deputy Bolan placed the phone in a clear bag and sealed it before tucking it in his pocket. Then he removed the glove. "I'm going to need to know where you're staying this weekend."

Bigsby's eyes popped with fear. "You're not going to arrest me, are you?"

"No, but I want to know where I can find you if I change my mind," the deputy said.

"We rented a house on Meadowlark Lane," he said.

"Number twenty," the middle werewolf chimed in. "Listen, I don't know what happened to Clark, but the three of us have been together nonstop. If Bigsby had done anything, we'd know about it."

The werewolf on the right swiveled in the vampire's direction. "You might want to talk to the heavy breather. The pixie came after us, but he was already here when we arrived. Maybe he put the phone there."

"My name isn't obiwandkenobi, is it?" the vampire asked. "Besides, don't you think I would've stolen all the supplies and gold for myself? Besides, if I were going to dispose of evidence, I wouldn't be foolish enough to stand next to it. No one was here when I arrived. I would've simply moved on to another location and no one would be the wiser."

Deputy Bolan ambled over to the vampire. "Is your name actually Vlad?"

"No, it's Stuart Mackenzie," the vampire said. "And if you must know, I'm staying at Casper's Revenge."

"Are you here alone?" the deputy asked.

"Look around, Deputy. I'm never alone at these tournaments."

"I'm Shelley," the pixie said. "I'm staying with my sister in the White Oak neighborhood."

"Did you know Clark?" I asked.

"Of course," Stuart said. "Anyone who's been attending these tournaments with regularity knows the leprechaun. He posts every screenshot of his achievements like he's curing cancer."

"Have you seen him since you've been in Starry Hollow?" I asked.

"No. Then again, he's rather small. I could easily have missed him." He flashed his fangs at the deputy. "No offense."

"You can't make something not offensive just by tacking 'no offense' to the end of the sentence," the deputy grumbled.

The vampire returned his attention to the screen and cheered. "Yes! Finally!"

The werewolves growled in protest.

"You don't know how long I've been trying to kill this one." He practically skipped away from the tree. "Best of luck, furballs. See you at the victory celebration…or not."

"Nobody leaves town until you get the all-clear from the sheriff or me," Deputy Bolan said. "Come on, Rose. I want to get this phone back to the office."

We retreated to the car and I watched as the werewolves slowly returned their attention to the game. At least they had the decency to look too stunned by the news to play for five minutes. They seemed to be in the minority.

As the leprechaun began to reverse down the dirt path, my focus shifted to the large ash tree. The sight of it filled me with a sense of dread. "What's the historical significance of the Tree of Bounty? I've never heard of it."

The leprechaun's face darkened. "That's a question better left to your coven."

"Why? Do they own it or something?"

He shifted uneasily. "Not exactly." He glanced at me sideways. "Should I drop you back at your car?"

"That would be good," I said. "I need to get Marley and feed her. She's probably putting a hex on me for abandoning her during the tournament. I want to know what you find on the phone though."

"You focus on your article and let the law enforcement professionals focus on the investigation," he said.

"Right. Like that ever happens," I said. "I'm in this until the bitter end, Deputy Bolan. There are way too many suspects running around town and only you and the sheriff to track them down. Face it, you need me." And if we didn't get to the bottom of this soon, somebody was going to win more than a tournament—they were going to get away with murder.

CHAPTER SIX

Marley and I arrived back at the cottage to find the front door ajar. "Wait here," I said. I pulled out my wand and nudged the door far enough for me to slip through the gap. Nothing seemed amiss. PP3 was sound asleep on the sofa, which was a good sign. If there was someone unwanted in the cottage, he would be expressing his displeasure. Loudly.

A noise in the kitchen diverted my attention there and I tiptoed toward the door. Slowly, I pushed it open and was greeted by the site of Raoul standing on the kitchen island with what appeared to be part of a tree trunk. He glanced up when he heard the door open.

"Raoul, why did you leave the front door open? You scared me half to death."

Marley appeared behind me with her wand brandished. "Is it safe? Are you dead yet?"

"False alarm," I said. I turned back to the raccoon. "Don't you know that someone was murdered in Linnea's kitchen this morning? It's really not a good idea to be breaking and entering right now. Or ever."

I wasn't breaking and entering. I'm your familiar. You should have sensed it was me.

"Sorry. I'm a little preoccupied thanks to Clark's murder." I moved closer to examine the tree trunk. "What is this and why is it in my kitchen?"

Somebody gave it to me at the dump, he said. *I mentioned that I was looking for a tree stump in good shape and voilà.*

"And what exactly is your plan for this tree stump?" I asked.

It was meant to be a surprise for you, but I guess that ship has sailed.

"Maybe next time try not hiding the surprise in my house."

Marley joined me at the island and examined the other objects next to the tree stump. "Are you learning woodworking, Raoul?" she asked.

Tell her these are going to be the legs. He gestured to spare pieces of wood next to the stump.

"He's adding these pieces as legs," I translated. I jerked back to him. "Egads, you're not trying to build me some kind of Pinocchio boyfriend, are you?"

Marley's blue eyes sparkled. "Are you making an altar?"

Raoul nudged me and pointed to Marley. *See? She gets it.*

I shook my head. "I don't understand. It looks like a stool."

"No," Marley said. She pointed to the candle and incense burner. "It's for you. A personal altar where you can read from the grimoire."

You can decorate it with whichever deities you want, Raoul said.

"Did you get all of these things at the dump?" I asked.

Why do you sound so surprised? The dump is basically paradise for random stuff.

"This is very sweet of you," I said. "Don't feel like you have to go out of your way for me though. I'm not sure how often I'm going to be standing at the altar in the cottage. I'm lucky to make it to the monthly coven meetings." I attended because I knew that if I didn't show up, Aunt Hyacinth would come looking for me to drag me there by the hair if necessary.

"Some of these things must've been hard to get," Marley said. "The incense burner looks brand-new."

The raccoon shrugged. *They were offered to me as gifts.*

"Which goddess do you want to have on your altar, Mom?" Marley asked. "I like that famous one of Venus."

"I think we'd better let Raoul finish making the altar first before we decorate it," I said. I wasn't sure I wanted to see a raccoon with a drill. Probably best if I avoided the work area that day.

I went to the refrigerator to find food for Marley and me. "I'm sorry I abandoned our plans to play. How did you and your friends make out? Were you able to complete any of the challenges?"

Marley took a seat at the table. "It was okay. We ran into a bunch of other players, but everyone else seems so serious. It kind of takes the fun out of it."

I gave her a sympathetic look. "Are you rethinking your goal to be a girl gamer?"

"I saw girls here and there, so I feel better about it." She fidgeted with her hair. "I also don't love the fact that the game involves killing. I know it isn't real, but I didn't feel very good whenever I killed a werewolf or a vampire."

I brought two glasses of dandelion iced tea to the table and offered one to Marley. "That's because you're a girl after my own heart."

"I don't know about that," Marley said. "You're from Jersey. You have violent tendencies."

"Only when someone is really aggravating and deserves it," I said diplomatically.

"Did my dad like these kinds of games?" she asked.

I was taken aback by the question. Marley rarely asked specific questions about her father.

I sat in the chair adjacent to hers. "He played casually, but it wasn't really his thing either. He used to listen to audiobooks in his truck, especially when he had long distance deliveries."

Marley lit up. "Really? I didn't know that. What kind of books did he like to listen to?"

"Mainstream stuff like Stephen King and John Grisham. Sometimes a Robert Ludlow book. The *Star Wars* books. He liked to keep his mind occupied while he drove. Otherwise, it was too monotonous." Karl didn't complain very often about his job, probably because he always took steps to improve whatever bothered him. It was one of his better qualities.

"Can I read Stephen King?" Marley asked.

"No," I said without hesitation.

Marley swallowed her iced tea. "Why not? If he's so popular, why do you think I won't like him?"

"Because I woke up this morning to find you in my bed after a bad dream again," I said. "You've made progress since we've moved here, and the last thing I'm going to do is set you back by putting *The Shining* in your trembling hands. Let's leave Mr. King until you're a bit older, please. For both of our sakes."

"Fine," Marley huffed.

I reached for an apple in the fruit bowl and passed it to her. "Have a snack and I'll make you a quick lunch. Dinner will be late because I'm going to go back out and talk to gamers about Clark."

Marley pulled out her wand and said, "*Scelerisque*." She

tapped the apple with her wand and a chocolate coating appeared.

"Marley Rose, what do you think you're doing?"

Marley smiled. "Making my apple edible?"

I stared at the chocolate-covered apple. "Did you learn this at school?"

"Sort of," she said. "I might have improvised a little."

I wasn't about to dissuade her from challenging herself. "Can you do one for me? Make it caramel, please." I plucked another apple from the bowl and set it on a napkin in front of me. Marley performed the spell again and I smiled with delight to see caramel dripping down the sides of my apple.

"That looks good," Marley said.

"Finally, a useful magic trick," I said. "This is what Hazel should be teaching me."

Raoul snickered. *Tell her you'll draw runes in the caramel coating.*

I licked some of the caramel off my apple. "I don't care what grade your teacher gives you, Marley. I give this spell an A+." I polished off the apple in record time and downed my iced tea before whipping together two sandwiches for lunch.

"I hate to eat and run, but I need to get back out there while the gamers are still wandering around town in full force."

"Should I come with you?" Marley asked.

"How would you feel about being left on your own for an hour or so?"

Marley chewed her lip. "Are you sure you'll only be an hour?" I could see the anxiety flaring.

"It's daytime. I thought you might want to give it a try." Sometimes she seemed eager to be more independent and other times she seemed to want to retreat into a childlike state. "I won't force you if you're not up for it."

I'll keep an eye on her, Raoul said. *I was planning to work on your altar anyway*.

Would you mind working on it in the back garden? I asked. *No offense, but the thought of leaving Marley alone with a raccoon and a tool doesn't sit well with me*.

Why not? You leave her with Alec all the time.

"Hardy har."

Oh, ye of little faith, Raoul said. *I can operate a drill*.

You don't even have opposable thumbs, I countered. *Forgive me if I lack confidence in your skills*.

PP3 began to bark in the other room. "Someone needs to go out," I said.

"I can take him," Marley said. "It'll give me a chance to check on my herb garden."

"After that, would you like to go and see Artemis?" I knew the elderly witch would be happy to keep Marley company while I worked. Her house would likely still be overrun with players anyway. Marley could join in if she wanted and I'd feel good about having Jefferson watch over her unseen. It would give the illusion of independence.

"What about Florian?" she asked. "Then you don't have to go out of your way."

"Florian is busy with the tournament," I said. "I can see if Mrs. Babcock is around, but she tends to be busy at Thornhold during the day."

"No, that's okay. I'd like to see Artemis and Jefferson." She giggled. "Not that I see Jefferson."

She can hang out with a ghost, but she can't read Stephen King, Raoul said.

The only thing creepy about Jefferson is his relationship with Artemis, I replied.

I'll take your word for it, the raccoon said.

My phone buzzed and I glanced down to see Magnus

Destry's name. I snatched the phone to my ear. "Hey, Slyther-claw. How's it going?"

"I finally had a chance to poke through the archives and I think you'll be quite interested in what I found."

"You found a file on Ivy?"

"I found better than that," he said. "I found the transcript of the meeting where she was removed from power as written by the coven's scribe at the time. Very detailed."

"Can I see it?"

"I'm afraid I can't remove the papers from the archival room," he said. "It's against coven rules."

"Can you screenshot them? Then you can just text to them to me. Nobody has to break any rules."

"There are a lot of papers here, Ember."

I drummed my fingers on the table. "Then what do you suggest?"

He was quiet for a moment. "How adept are you with invisibility spells?"

Excitement stirred within me. "I can do that! When do you want me there?"

"How about now? No one's around."

"I'll be there as soon as I can."

"Who was that?" Marley asked.

"I'll tell you when I have more information," I said. I had a premade sachet for an invisibility spell in the pantry, so I hurried to put it in my pocket. Unfortunately, I wasn't going to be able to brag to my tutors about this because I couldn't let them know I was using the spell to break into the archival room. Stupid scruples.

I dropped Marley at Haverford House and drove straight to Silver Moon headquarters. I activated the spell so that no one saw me enter.

"Hey, girl," I said, as I passed beneath the witch statue at the top of the building.

Magnus was right. The building seemed deserted. I bypassed the cavernous hall where we held our monthly coven meetings and headed toward the staircase that led to the lower level.

The coven definitely gave more attention to the main level than the underground rooms. The corridor was dimly lit with a low ceiling and a damp chill. I wanted to call for Magnus, but didn't want to risk revealing my presence in case someone else was within earshot. Just because they couldn't see me didn't mean they couldn't identify my voice.

I spotted Magnus lingering in the doorway of a room at the end of the corridor. He was as glued to his phone as the players in the game. When I was certain the coast was clear, I sidled up to him.

"Why aren't you participating in the tournament?" I asked.

He jumped and scowled at me. "A little warning next time, please."

I smothered a laugh. "Sorry. It was too good to pass up."

"I'm a devoted auror in Wizards Unite. I don't have time for other games. Perhaps next time your cousins will arrange an event for the superior game." He tucked his phone into his cloak pocket. "This way."

I trailed behind him as we passed by rows of filing cabinets. "You don't have the transcript out and ready?"

"I couldn't risk it in case someone came in," he said. "Not to worry. I know exactly where to find it." He rounded a corner and I followed.

"They certainly put it in the deepest, darkest recesses of the archives," I said.

"Not an accident, I'm sure." He stopped at the end unit and twirled his wand to open the top drawer. An unmarked brown folder floated down into his waiting hands.

"How did you find it?" I asked. "There's nothing to identify it on the outside."

"I used a spell, of course," he said. He frowned. "I want to hand this to you, but I don't know where you are."

I plucked the folder from his hand and opened it. The notes were lengthy and dense.

"I must warn you," he said. "The notes of the meeting are detailed, but don't tell you the whole story, if that makes sense."

"You mean they were cautious about what they said during the meeting," I said. The coven knew this would be the official record of the proceedings. They likely chose their words carefully to protect themselves from later scrutiny.

"It was an unprecedented event," Magnus said. "Never before had a High Priestess been forced to step down."

"You forgot the worst part," I said. "I don't think Ivy would've minded the High Priestess part. It was losing her magic that would've been the most upsetting."

I skimmed the pages of small script. Gardenia didn't realize how fortunate she was to record coven activities with technology instead of writing by hand.

"They torpedoed her with questions," I said. "Sometimes Ivy's answers don't seem connected to the questions."

"No surprise there. The coven believed her immense power was impacting her mental state. You can see references to that in the transcript."

As I continued to read, I could practically feel Ivy's anguish in her responses. It must've been heartbreaking to feel that your own kind—your magical family—had turned against you.

I began to skip the questions and focus only on Ivy's answers. Some of the words weren't in English. They weren't in Latin either, but I didn't recognize them. There was something almost rhythmic about them.

"Do you know which language she's mixing in?"

Magnus glanced at the transcript. "I assumed they were the ravings of a lunatic."

"You don't really believe that the intensity of her magic drove her crazy, do you?" I asked.

Magnus puckered his lips, debating. "No, I think it was more likely that the coven wished to present her that way to justify their actions."

"I knew you were a conspiracy theorist at heart."

"A concentration of power makes others uncomfortable," he said. "It's a natural reaction."

"Is that why you're not a fan of Aunt Hyacinth? Because you think she's too powerful in Starry Hollow?"

"Make no mistake, Ember. Your aunt isn't even on the same continent as Ivy Rose in terms of power."

Maybe that was the point. Maybe my aunt longed for the power that Ivy had and that was the reason she'd hoarded Ivy's possessions all these years.

"That being said," he continued, "I have an innate distrust of anyone with too much influence." He waved a hand. "Power corrupts and absolute power corrupts absolutely and all that."

"You really do sound like Sheriff Nash," I said. "He can't stand that my aunt has any influence in town when she doesn't hold an official title."

"The Council of Elders is hardly unofficial," Magnus said.

"They're not elected or held accountable to anyone either," I said.

"Trust me, if they ever veered out of line, I feel confident that there would be strong objections."

I turned my attention back to Ivy's answers. I set the folder on a nearby table and pulled out my phone. Every time I encountered a random word that seemed to have no connection to the text, I typed it into my notes app. By the time I'd been through the entire transcript, I had a list of twenty-five unfamiliar words.

"Do you think these are all the same language?" I asked.

Magnus peered at the list. "Quite possibly. You'll have to research each one to know for certain though."

"Easy enough," I said. Marley would help me. She'd love to tackle a mini-project like this one.

"I'm sorry the transcript wasn't more illuminating," he said. "When I saw the length of it, I assumed there would be more actual information."

I put away my phone and returned the folder to the wizard. "Thanks, Magnus. You're a rock star."

I had a feeling there was more here than either of us realized. Ivy hadn't only given answers to the coven's questions, I was fairly certain that she'd given me the answers to mine as well.

CHAPTER SEVEN

I DECIDED to stop by the *Vox Populi* office to research the words on the list I'd made from Ivy's ramblings. I sailed through the front door, singing to myself, and was surprised to see Bentley hunched over his desk.

He glanced up sharply. "Who's there?"

I realized I was still invisible and removed the sachet from my pocket.

Bentley tipped his chair backward and nearly fell. "Stars and stones, Ember! Are you trying to kill me?"

"No, but now I know how to go about it." I shook the sachet.

"Why are you doing an invisibility spell?" he asked. He gave me the once-over. "Oh, I see. You haven't showered today."

I glared at him. "I showered. I even combed my hair when it was still wet."

Bentley shrugged. "Okay then. I've got nothing."

"What are you doing here?" I asked.

"I should ask the same of you," Bentley replied. "It's Saturday. You don't even come in here on the days you're supposed to."

I stuck out my tongue and took my seat at the desk next to his. "Do you ever clean up? Who needs that many pencils in this day and age? Don't you type everything as it is?"

Bentley placed a protective hand over his mess of pencils. "I like to kick it old school when it comes to my journalism."

I choked on laughter. "Bentley, you're like the Charlie Brown of kicking it old school."

"I have no idea what that means."

The door burst open and Deputy Bolan stumbled in. I resisted the urge to laugh at his comical entrance.

"One too many shamrock shakes today?" I asked.

He eyed me angrily. "Someone needs to fix that."

Bentley and I exchanged amused glances. "Fix what?" I asked.

He pointed to the threshold. "There's a bump there. It's a trip hazard."

"Maybe for your dainty feet," I said. "The rest of us manage to get in and out of here on a regular basis without injury."

"I have an update on the victim's phone," the leprechaun said. "I thought you might want to know."

My eyes rounded. "You're willingly sharing information with me?" Not only that, but he must've tracked me here. I rarely showed up in the office on a Saturday.

Bentley smirked. "He must need help with something. What is it, Deputy Bolan? Is technology stumping you?"

Deputy Bolan pressed his thin lips together. "I need to find obiwandkenobi and I can't figure out how."

"Sheriff Nash couldn't help you?" I asked.

"He's out on duty. This tournament is causing traffic issues in a few places. Players keep stopping in the middle of the road to complete their challenges and we've had a few near misses."

Bentley held out his hand and wiggled his fingers. "Give it here. Let the expert assist you."

I rolled my eyes. "Expert might be a bit strong." Then again, the elf managed to meet his wife through the magic of technology. Maybe he was more of an expert than I gave him credit for.

Bentley flicked through the screens. "They're friends on the game. You only need to click on the map icon and it should show us the user's location."

"Wait," I said. "I thought you could only check your friends' progress in the game. You can check their locations too?"

"Sure," Bentley said. "There's a tracking system built in."

I cringed. We could've found Clark's phone much earlier if we'd known. It seemed I was as inept with technology as magic, not that this was news as someone that regularly blew up the microwave.

Deputy Bolan came to stand beside Bentley to peer at the map. "Looks like the woods not far from Fairy Cove."

Bentley clicked back to the game and scrolled to that location. "There's a water dragon in that vicinity."

The deputy's own phone pinged and he snatched it from his pocket to read the text. "Oh, great."

"What is it?" I asked.

"A fight broke out between players at the dock and the sheriff is already dealing with a crowd control issue near the fountain." He shook his head. "I can't wait for this tournament to be over."

"I'll track down obiwandkenobi," I said.

"I'll go too," Bentley said.

Deputy Bolan blew out a breath. "Don't do anything

stupid. Just pretend you want to interview him for the newspaper."

I gave him a mock salute. "You can count on us, Mr. Deputy, sir."

He snarled and snatched the victim's phone from Bentley's hand. "I'll keep the evidence, thanks."

"Now you know how to find Lewis," I said. "His user name is gardendelight."

Deputy Bolan tapped the phone against his temple. "Good thinking, Rose. That'll be next on the list after I break up this fight...I hope."

I waited for Bentley to shut down his computer and gather his belongings.

"I'll drive," I said.

"As long as you promise not to sing," Bentley said. "My ears function better when they're not bleeding."

I plucked the pointy tip of his ear. "And here I thought these were purely decorative."

Although the drive only took five minutes, there was no way to park nearby, so we ended up walking another ten minutes through the woods to get there. We found obiwandkenobi wandering the cliff overlooking Fairy Cove. The goblin wore a brown hooded cape and had a light saber hooked to his belt. He was with a friend—a dwarf in a white hooded cape with a rope belt. Unsurprisingly, they were tapping and swiping on their screens with abandon and failed to notice our arrival.

"Help me, obiwandkenobi," I said. "You're my only hope."

The goblin and dwarf stopped playing and gaped at me like I'd just emerged naked from the sea on an oyster shell.

"Dude, she quotes *Stars Wars*," the dwarf said in awe.

"Will you marry me?" the goblin asked, appearing completely sincere.

Bentley snickered. "I think I'll leave this one to you."

"I think you would anyway because you have no idea what you're doing," I shot back. I inched closer to the players. "Guys, that's a line that everybody knows. You don't even need to be a super fan to know that one."

"Are you, though?" the goblin asked, his hope evident. "A super fan of *Star Wars*?"

"I'm more of a casual fan," I admitted. "I don't have a nervous breakdown and threaten to storm Skywalker Ranch when my favorite character does something I dislike." Karl, however, had been a huge fanboy. I could only imagine what his reaction would have been to the later films.

"You've suddenly become less attractive," the goblin said.

"Right back at you," I said. "My name is Ember Rose and this is my associate, Bentley Smith. We're writing an article about the tournament for the local paper and would like to ask you a few questions."

"You want to interview us?" The dwarf's shining excitement was priceless. "Nobody ever wants to talk to us. I'm lucky if someone says excuse me when they burp at me."

I felt a twinge of guilt over the deception. If the goblin wasn't the killer, I'd make sure to include these two in an article and even include a photograph.

"Let's start simple. What are your names?" Bentley asked. He took out his phone, ready to take notes.

"I'm Darth Nugent," the dwarf said.

"Your *real* names," I said.

"That is his real name," the goblin said. "He had it legally changed two years ago." They fist bumped. "An epic decision."

"And are you General Zod?" I asked.

All three males looked ready to slap me. Bentley found his voice first. "Zod is from Superman," he said in a clipped tone.

"I know," I lied. "I was just making up a name. I should have said General Palpatine."

"Emperor Palpatine," they said in unison.

"You've gone from hero to zero in record time," the goblin said.

"As long as it's a record," I said. "I like to win. I bet you do, too, Mr...."

"Patton Bismark," said the goblin.

"How's the game?" I asked. "Are you killing lots of dragons? There's a water dragon here, right?"

"Patton's doing better than I am," Darth Nugent said. "He was able to buy a flaming crossbow which totally helped him defeat the ice dragon."

"Are flaming crossbows hard to come by?" I asked.

"They're expensive," Patton said. "Took most of my gold for that purchase, but it was worth it."

"How did you manage to get so much more gold than your friend?" I asked. "Haven't you been playing together the whole time?"

They exchanged wary glances.

"I got lucky," Patton said. "Got a windfall earlier today."

"Oh, really?" I asked. "How'd you manage that?"

The goblin rocked on the balls of his feet. "Someone donated it to me."

"Wow, that does sound lucky," I said. I turned to Bentley. "I sure wish someone would donate a pot of gold to me."

"It's not a pot," Bentley said. "You're thinking of leprechauns."

"As a matter of fact, I am," I said. I shifted back to the pair of players. "Did you get the gold from a leprechaun, by any chance, Patton?"

The goblin's eyes rounded. "I don't know. His user name is cleverclover. I guess that sounds leprechaun-ish."

"Someone you don't know donated so much gold to you that you could buy a flaming crossbow?" I asked.

The goblin's head bobbed up and down.

I faced Bentley. "What's the penalty for stealing gold in the game?"

"Public beheading," Bentley replied, completely serious.

"I didn't steal it," Patton blurted. "It just showed up in my account, I swear."

"And you didn't question it?" I asked. "Are players typically that generous?"

Patton glanced helplessly at his friend. "No, but what was I going to do? Hunt the guy down and ask why he did it? I have a game to play!"

I peered at him. "Maybe he didn't donate it to you. Maybe you had cleverclover's phone and used it to transfer the gold to your own account."

Patton blinked his bulbous goblin eyes. "Why would I have someone else's phone?"

Because you killed him and stole it.

"Because Clark is the front runner and you want to win," I said, echoing the statement of the werewolf trio.

Patton gave an adamant shake of his head. "No, I would never do that."

"He wouldn't," Darth Nugent chimed in. "He won't even take coins from under the sofa cushions. He gives them to his grandma whenever he finds them. Besides, I was with him when he got the gold. He was totally shocked."

"So, you admit to being an accessory?" Bentley asked with a little too much enthusiasm.

The dwarf glared at him. "Do I look like a necklace to you?"

"Darth and I were slaying dragons," Patton said. "It was like magic. I'd made it to the ice dragon, but the dragon killed me and came back stronger. None of my weapons were powerful enough."

"And then the gold appeared out of nowhere," Darth said. "It was a Wizards Connect miracle."

It was entirely possible that Patton had pretended that the gold had inexplicably appeared when he knew it had been there since this morning.

"There's no way to use a spell on the game, right?" I asked. "No one can add gold to their account using magic?"

"No, the game designers made it magic-proof," Darth said. "You might want to mention that in your article. Don't want to attract cheaters to the game."

I needed to find out more information on Patton's movements over the weekend without letting him know about the investigation. I'd already put him on alert in connection with the gold, so I had to proceed with caution or I risked losing his cooperation.

"Bentley, don't you think it would be interesting to follow a player like Patton from the start of the game to the end?"

The dwarf raised his hand. "And me. I'd be interesting too. Okay, well not really because I'm pretty boring, but it would be cool to be included."

I had to admit that I was quickly developing a soft spot for the dwarf. "Yes, definitely. Anyone who changes their name to one of my favorite *Star Wars* characters needs his time in the spotlight."

Darth gave his friend a smug look.

"I thought Princess Leia would be your favorite," Bentley said.

"Why? Because she's the token female?" I asked.

Bentley shrugged. "Well, yeah."

"Actually, Yoda is my favorite, followed by Darth Vader," I said. "I have a thing for men in black."

"Darth and I prepped last night," Patton said. "We went around town and tried to get a handle on the hot spots."

"A lot of us do it," Darth said. "That way we don't spend time getting lost during the tournament. It's impossible to locate all the spots in advance, but it gives you an edge."

That explained the players lurking at Palmetto House before the start of the tournament.

Bentley stopped typing on his phone and looked at them. "Have you two been together from the start until now?"

"Pretty much," Darth said.

"Well, we don't sleep or shower together or anything," Patton added quickly.

"Not that there's anything wrong with that," Darth said. "And we haven't spent *all* our time together. We split up this morning."

My radar pinged. "What time?"

Darth cut a quick glance at his friend. "Early, wasn't it? You went to get coffee around five-thirty, I think."

"No, I didn't," Patton said. His cheeks turned pink.

"You did," Darth said. "Because I asked you to get me a peppermint latte and you told me no, that I'd be better off mixing my toothpaste in milk, remember?"

"Where did you go for coffee?" I asked.

Patton suddenly took great interest in the dirt beneath his feet. "The coffee shop," he mumbled.

"Which one?" I pressed.

Patton met my penetrating gaze. "The one that sells… coffee. How should I know? I don't live here."

"Do you have a receipt?" I asked.

"No, I paid cash and told them I didn't need one," Patton said.

Bentley fixed him with a hard stare. "Can you describe the interior? Color scheme? The barista?"

"The barista was…pretty," Patton said.

"Well, that rules out the Caffeinated Cauldron," Bentley muttered.

Patton pointed at us excitedly. "Yes, that was the name."

"Was it busy when you were there?" I asked.

"Not really," he said. "I got my drink pretty fast."

"What did you order?" Bentley asked.

Patton seemed to stumble over his answer. "A plain coffee. With cream." He hesitated. "Not sugar."

Darth laughed. "Dude, I don't know why you decided to suddenly take up coffee. It sounds like you don't even know how to order it."

I kept my focus on the squirming goblin. "You're not a regular coffee drinker?"

"No, but I figured I'd need it with the early starts this weekend. I've been tired."

If Patton arrived at the coffee shop before six and it wasn't busy, he still might have had time to kill Clark at Palmetto House. They were within walking distance from each other.

"Hey, would you mind if I add you guys as friends on the game?" I asked. "Not that I'll catch up to you, but I can keep tabs on your progress…for the article."

"Awesome," Darth said. "Just search for our user names and send the request."

I flashed a smile. "Got it."

"For what it's worth, I still think you're pretty hot," Patton said.

"I'm almost twice your age and not remotely interested," I said.

His face slackened. "You just got even hotter."

"Dude, you can't drool," Darth Nugent said. "You might mess up your phone."

Patton wiped his mouth with his sleeve.

"Good luck with the game, guys," I said. I linked my arm through Bentley's and steered him back through the woods toward the car. "For the first time ever, I wouldn't have objected to you kissing me." Anything to stave off their interest in me.

Bentley recoiled. "Yes, but I most certainly would have."

"Don't be such a baby. You would've liked it. There might have even been tongue involved."

He cringed. "You're weirdly aggressive right now."

"It's the game," I said. "I think I have an untapped competitive streak, which is strange because I'm also lazy."

"What do we do now?" he asked.

"*We* are doing nothing," I said. "*I*, on the other hand, have a sudden hankering for a latte."

And a few questions for the barista.

CHAPTER EIGHT

I ARRIVED at the Caffeinated Cauldron not sure what to expect. The coffee shop appeared to have the usual number of patrons for a Saturday afternoon. Nobody was zipping back for refills, it seemed. It made sense. Once these players were in the zone, they probably didn't want to break their stride by taking a coffee break.

I walked straight up to the counter and greeted Riley, the barista. The pixie was relatively new as the coffee shop suffer from a steady turnover of employees.

"How's the weekend going so far?" I asked. "I bet the tournament is keeping you on your toes."

"You have no idea," Riley said. "We were crazy busy this morning from the moment we unlocked the doors. We had a line out the door and everybody wanted extra large cups. I can't wait to go home and crash."

Inwardly, I sighed. If they were that busy this morning, then Patton had lied. I'd hoped the goblin had been telling the truth.

"Do you recall seeing a goblin in line this morning?" I

asked. "He'd be hard to miss. He was wearing a brown hooded robe and carrying a light saber."

The barista laughed. "I'd definitely remember that. No, the only Dark Side referenced here was in relation to coffee."

I was more disappointed than I cared to admit. I kind of liked Patton and Darth's goofy demeanors. I hated the idea of the goblin killing Clark. Then again, maybe it was provoked. I'd only spent a dinner with the leprechaun and I could totally understand wanting to knock him on the head with something hard and heavy—not that I was making excuses for the killer.

"Were you the only one working?" I asked.

"No, I called for reinforcements when I saw the line forming," she said. She craned her neck to call to the berserker behind her. "Hey, A.J., did you see anyone here this morning in *Star Wars* gear?"

A.J. smiled. "No, but I wish I had. Would've made my day."

"Would you mind checking your morning receipts for a plain coffee with cream and no sugar? It would have been between five-thirty and six."

"Well, we don't get many of those," Riley said. "Should be easy enough." She sprinkled pixie dust on the screen in front of her and studied the results. "No, sorry. I had a flat white at six-thirty, but that's the closest."

"Thanks," I said. Dread coiled in my stomach. I was going to have to let the sheriff and deputy know. Poor Darth wouldn't know what to do with himself without his constant companion.

I left the coffee shop and hurried to the sheriff's office to let him know about my discovery. Sheriff Nash was back from his crowd control issue at the fountain and in the conference room with the door closed. I paced the length of the waiting area, keeping myself entertained by practicing incantations. Wren would be proud of me—except for the part where I accidentally extinguished all the leaves off one of the plants. I tried in vain to reverse the spell.

"Rose, what are you doing out here?"

"Waiting for you," I said, and jumped in front of the plant. "I have information about the case."

Two minotaurs left the conference room. "Thanks for your help, gentlemen," the sheriff said. "I'll be in touch. Remember not to leave town."

The two minotaurs breezed past me without a glance. Their phones were already out and pressed to their noses. Two more players eager to return to the game.

The sheriff frowned. "Have you done something out here?"

"What do you mean?" I asked, feigning innocence.

"I don't know. Something looks different in here. I can't quite put my finger on it."

I shuffled forward, trying to keep my body positioned directly in front of the plant remains. "I spoke to a suspect earlier and his alibi doesn't check out."

He cocked an eyebrow. "Who is it?"

"Patton, the goblin who inherited the gold," I said.

The sheriff nodded and stroked his stubbled chin. "Oh, obiwandkenobi."

"He seems kind of sweet, so I'm actually surprised," I said.

"You think because someone seems sweet, they can't be guilty of murder? That doesn't sound like the Jersey girl I know."

"No, that's not what I mean. I guess I don't get a killer vibe from him, that's all. He wears a *Star Wars* robe and carries a light saber. He probably has C-3PO underwear on."

"But he lied about his alibi and he has all the gold from Clark's account?" Sheriff Nash offered a sad smile. "Sounds like we need to have another talk with our young Jedi."

"I think I can find him," I said. "I added him as a friend on the game so I could track him if I needed to."

The sheriff squeezed my shoulder. "Look at you, Rose. Thinking ahead."

"Right? If I could apply this to my domestic duties, I'd always have an answer to 'what's for dinner?'" I said. I took out my phone and opened the app. "According to the map, he's…" I peered at the screen. Okay, now was an embarrassing moment to admit I wasn't a skilled map reader.

"What's the matter, Rose?"

I glanced up to see the werewolf grinning. "The map is…broken."

His grin broadened. "Broken, is it? Here, why don't I take a look and see if I can fix it?"

Reluctantly, I handed him the phone. Map reading fell by the wayside when you had a soothing lady's voice telling you which roads to take and where to turn. The only danger was that her voice was so calming that I risked slipping into a coma.

The sheriff pretended to tinker with the phone. "There. Now it's perfect." He returned the phone. "According to the blinking dot, I think we'll find him at the Burger Boggart."

"I guess he's one of those players that eats meals," I said. "A rare breed."

"Yeah, those minotaurs I questioned were loaded with protein bars and energy drinks. They weren't too happy about stopping to answer questions."

"I was wondering who they were," I said. "I guess you cleared them."

"Yep. Alibis and no motive." He started toward the door and I cut in front of him.

"I'm driving this time."

He bit back a smile. "Just to prove to me that you can?"

"I don't have to prove anything. I know I can," I said. "I just think it'll be fun to annoy you."

"Good grief," the sheriff said. "Why do I put up with this abuse?"

I laughed as I sailed out the door. "Because you..." I stopped myself before I said something stupid. "Because you're a fool."

"That I am, Rose. No arguments here."

An awkward silence settled over us until I started the car and turned on the magic radio. "Play Billy Joel's *Big Shot*."

The music began and Sheriff Nash winced at the sound. "I suppose I owe you," he said.

I sang along as loudly as I could with the windows down, banging on the steering wheel at appropriate points in the song. The sheriff observed me with a twinkle of amusement in his brown eyes.

I pulled into the parking lot of the Burger Boggart and made him wait until the song was finished before I turned off the engine. Only then did I roll up the windows.

"You've got quite a voice there, Rose. I imagine we lost a few animals along the way. May they rest in peace."

"You're just jealous because I'm willing to let loose and not worry about how I'll sound to others."

"Oh, you're clearly not worried about how you sound to others," he said.

"You shouldn't worry about how you sound," I said. "The joy is in the singing, not the listening."

He shot me a quizzical look. "If I were worried about how I sound to others, I never would've done karaoke."

"That was one time," I said. "It's not like you're regularly belting out tunes for public consumption."

"I don't think either one of us should be doing that," the sheriff said. "Might fall under cruel and unusual punishment."

We vacated the car and entered the Burger Boggart. I spotted Patton and Darth in a booth. Their plates were nearly empty and they were preoccupied with their phones.

I sidled up to the table. "Howdy, boys. Darth, why don't you take a walk? The sheriff and I need a word with your friend." When I saw the fear reflected in Patton's eyes, I almost felt sorry for him.

Darth surveyed the restaurant. "Where should I go? To the bathroom?"

"Sure. Or outside to scope out girls. I saw a pretty pixie out there with her hair in a bun." Okay, it wasn't two buns on the sides of her head but close enough.

Darth hustled from the table like we'd lit the booth on fire. I slid across from Patton and the sheriff sat beside me. I slotted my fingers together and gave the goblin a hard look.

"Why did you lie about the coffee shop?" I asked. Patton opened his mouth and I held up a hand. "No more lies. The next words out of your mouth need to be the truth or the sheriff is going to have to throw you in a cell. Right now, the sheriff's office is busy because of the tournament. Lots of disorderly conduct and muscled minotaurs crammed in cells together. Trust me, that's not where obiwandkenobi wants to be. Understand?"

"And we'd have to confiscate your light saber," the sheriff added.

Patton gulped. "Okay, okay. I wasn't getting coffee this morning."

"No kidding," I said. "Where were you?"

He made a soft, whining sound. "I was…doing sunrise yoga."

Not the answer I expected to hear. I leaned forward and cupped my hand to my ear. "I'm sorry. What was that?"

"I've been trying to be more present and mindful in my daily life. Games take me away from that, so I make an effort during high intensity times like tournaments to seek out yoga classes to keep me grounded and reduce stress." His cheeks were tinged with color again. "I've only been doing it for about six months, but it's made a big difference to my attitude and general mindset. I think it's had the added benefit of making me a better player too."

"And why is this a secret?" I asked.

The goblin stared at the plate in front of him. "I can't tell Darth and our other friends I'm doing yoga. They'd never let me live it down."

"So you lied to Darth about where you went this morning," I said. "And to me."

He rubbed his temples. "I know it was stupid. I froze. In the moment, it seemed the lesser of two dark sides."

"Is yoga really that uncool?" Sheriff Nash asked. "I thought it was pretty mainstream now."

"Not for goblins," he said. "And definitely not for my crew." He tapped on the prongs of his fork and nearly knocked it off the table as a result.

"Where did you go for yoga this morning?" Sheriff Nash asked.

"I met a group of witches. One of them is a big deal in the coven." He knocked on the table, thinking. "Some kind of flower."

"That doesn't really narrow it down in the Silver Moon coven," I said.

He lit up. "Iris. Her name was Iris."

I glanced at the sheriff. "I think he's telling the truth. Iris Sandstone teaches a yoga class."

"We're going to check with her all the same," the sheriff said.

Patton nodded quickly. "I swear on my light saber. It's the truth."

"And what about the gold?" I asked. "Did you find Clark's phone and dispose of it after you transferred the assets?"

"There's no need to lie, Patton," the sheriff said in a reassuring voice. "If your alibi checks out, we know you're innocent and it would be really helpful to know where you found the phone."

The goblin licked his lips. "I didn't find the phone. I'm sorry. I wish I could say I saw something helpful, but I swear the stuff just showed up in my account. I was too ecstatic to care about how it happened."

A thought flashed in my mind. "Have you had any arguments with anyone at the tournament?"

Patton shrank back. "Me?"

"I hate to be Captain Obvious, but he's not the dead one, Rose."

"No, but someone transferred Clark's gold to Patton in an attempt to incriminate him. Maybe the killer was settling two scores."

The goblin blew out an anxious breath. "I can't think of anyone. Darth and I mostly keep to ourselves. We haven't interacted with a lot of players…" He stopped abruptly. "Hang on, there was that girl that made fun of my outfit when Darth and I were checking out the hot spots yesterday."

"If everyone who made fun of your outfit was responsible for murder, we'd have a massacre on our hands," I said.

Patton squirmed in his seat. "No, seriously. It was more than that. I mentioned that I couldn't swim and she threatened to push me off the dock to see if the Force would rescue me." He made a dismissive noise. "She obviously has no understanding of how the Force works."

"She sounds delightful," I said. "What's her name?"

"I think it's Nova," Patton said. "At least that was the name on her backpack. She's a banshee. Just follow the trail of wincing werewolves and you'll find her. Her voice is pretty awful."

"What caused your altercation?" the sheriff asked.

Patton lowered his gaze. "She might have overheard me say something unkind to Darth about her voice. That it sounded like someone was strangling a dolphin while raking their nails down a chalkboard."

"That's quite the comparison," I said. "I can see why it might have annoyed her."

"I didn't expect her to hear me," the goblin said. "She threatened to take my light saber and shove it…"

I held up a hand. "We get the picture."

"Any chance you know her user name in the game?" the sheriff asked.

Patton scratched his head. "No. We're not friends. I've never seen her at a tournament before. This might be her first one."

"And, hopefully, you'll never see her again," I said.

"Thanks for being forthcoming, Patton," the sheriff said. "Until I clear your story with Iris, though, I need to ask you not to leave town."

"Okay, cool. I like this town. I don't mind hanging around after the tournament, but I hope you find the killer soon. If someone's targeting players, it might set off a wave of paranoia."

"It seems to be an isolated case so far," the sheriff said. "And Clark was a known winner, so more incentive to bump him off."

"Just out of curiosity," I began, "do you wear your robe for yoga?" For some reason, the mental image of obiwandkenobi performing sunrise yoga in his hooded cloak with a light saber filled me with unexpected joy.

Patton tugged the ends of the cloak together. "I only take it off to shower."

"Do you have a spare, so you can wash them?" The mother was strong in me.

"Rose, why don't we stay focused?" the sheriff suggested.

Patton edged his way out of the booth. "If that's all you need from me, I'm going to the register to pay. I want to get back to the game."

"Have fun," the sheriff said. "Slay a dragon or whatever it is you folks are doing."

Once Patton was out of earshot, I turned to the sheriff. "I have Iris in my contacts if you want to call," I said.

The werewolf gave me a wry smile. "I'm the sheriff, Rose. I've got the High Priestess in my contacts too. I've got almost every notable resident in here in case of emergency."

"Even Alec?" I asked.

"I said notable, not arrogant." He squeezed his eyes closed. "Sorry, Rose. I didn't mean that."

"Yes, you did, but that's okay. You're entitled to your opinion."

He tapped his screen and called Iris. I decided to text Alec while I waited and see whether he'd be finished with work early enough to see each other tonight. The vampire had been hyperfocused on his book lately and I was trying to give him the space he needed.

Whitethorn, tonight? I typed.

Not sure yet, he replied. *Stuck in a chapter*.

Anything I can do to help you get unstuck? I paused. *That was meant to sound flirty. I'm not very good at sexting*. Maybe there was a class I could take for that. I bet Florian was a decent sexter, not that I wanted tips from my cousin.

"His alibi checks out," the sheriff said, snapping me back to reality. "Iris said she didn't know his name, but that he was impossible to forget."

"Because of his outfit?" I asked.

"No, because he practically fell off the side of the cliff after mountain pose. Apparently, he's not very coordinated."

"All the more reason to do yoga then."

He glanced at the phone still in my hand. "Did I interrupt something?"

"No, no. Just killing time until you finished."

"That's what she said," he quipped.

I gave him a disapproving look. "Seriously?"

"Yeah, you're right. That's not my kind of humor." He slid out of the booth. "Time to track down the next suspect."

"Apparently, you're the litmus test. When your ears explode, we know we're in range of Nova."

"Great," he said, less than enthused. "Looking forward to meeting her."

"Hey, if she's our killer, then your temporary pain will have been worth it."

He gestured to the wand tucked in my purse. "Can't you magic me some earplugs?"

I cringed. "I burned all the leaves off your plant earlier. I can only imagine what I'd do to your appendages."

He shot a quick glance down at his lap. "On second thought, I'll pass on the earplugs."

I couldn't help but smile. "Thought you might say that."

CHAPTER NINE

DESPITE OUR INQUIRIES, nobody seemed to know Nova or a banshee participating in the tournament. Given the ratio of males to females, I would've thought a banshee would be memorable. Aster checked the roster of registered players for a Nova but there was no one by that name.

"We're sure she's a player this weekend and not a resident, right?" I asked. Sheriff Nash and I had left the Burger Boggart and were now lingering in the parking lot in front of the sheriff's office.

"According to our records, there's no Nova in Starry Hollow," the sheriff said. "She must be flying under the radar."

"Seems like something a killer might do," I said.

"My thoughts exactly." Sheriff Nash raked a hand through his thick hair.

"There's also the chance that Patton was wrong about her name," I said.

The sheriff shrugged. "It's all we have to go on. I've sent her name and description to Bolan to be on the lookout." He cut a glance at me. "You know, a little magic might go a long way right now."

I perked up. "What kind of magic?"

"Any chance you could do a locator spell—or do I need to ask a real witch?"

I reeled back. "Bite your tongue, Mr. Sheriff. Consider the gauntlet thrown."

"Can you really do one? If you can't, it's okay, Rose. I'm happy to ask someone else from the coven."

"Yes, yes. Your girlfriend Iris is on speed dial. I got it." I took a moment to consider whether I actually could perform a locator spell on Nova. Although I fully recognized that I wasn't yet the skilled witch Aunt Hyacinth wanted me to be, my ego couldn't handle appearing inferior to the sheriff.

"It's nothing personal, Rose. It would obviously be easier for me if you could do it since you're already part of the investigation."

"To be honest, I don't know if anyone can do a spell like that without a personal connection to Nova," I said. "It's not like we have a strand of her hair or anything."

A slow smile spread across the sheriff's face. "No, but I bet I know where I can get one. How about I track him down while you get set up at the cottage and I'll meet you there?"

I whipped out my phone. "Allow me to use the magic of technology to tell you exactly where our Force-loving friend is right now." I clicked on the game map. "You can find him at Balefire Beach."

"Perfect. I'll see you shortly."

I held up my hand for a high-five. "Woot! No weak links in this teamwork chain!"

The sheriff slapped my hand. "Nope."

We divided so that we could conquer. I drove back to the cottage and found Raoul and PP3 on the floor with an empty box.

"What on earth?" I stared at the powdered dust all over the floor. "Were those donuts?"

'Were' is the pertinent word in that question, Raoul said.

I bent down to examine the dog. "Did PP3 eat any of them?"

They were mini donuts and he only ate a couple.

"How can you be sure?" I asked.

Because I'd already eaten the rest.

My hands cemented to my hips. "You know this is going to probably give him diarrhea, right?"

Raoul sucked in a breath. *Ooh, that's nasty.*

"No kidding. And if that happens, guess who's going to be cleaning it up?"

He tapped a claw on his chin. *I don't know much about dogs. Does he lick it up himself?*

I shot him a warning glance. "Raoul…"

The raccoon offered a weak smile. *If a dog has diarrhea in the woods, does anybody really hear it?*

"He's not going to have it in the woods and who cares who hears it?"

It was meant to be a philosophical question.

"Okay, I don't have time for this. I need to get stuff ready before the sheriff gets here."

Raoul fixed his beady eyes on me. *Wait. Sexy time with the sheriff? I is confused.*

"Not sexy times. Locator spell time. I need to prove I'm a decent enough witch to help him track a suspect."

You're right. That's not sexy at all…Unless you wear a low-cut dress and thigh-high boots while you do it. Make sure you lean over the candle far enough so that…

I rolled my eyes. "I burn my nipples? I'm trying to catch a killer, not chlamydia."

You seem to be confusing the sheriff with his brother.

"I didn't really mean that Granger…" PP3 perked up and

began to bark. I shook a finger at my familiar. "No more talk about STIs in front of the sheriff."

Raoul held up a paw. *Need I remind you that he can't hear me?*

"No, but I can." I yanked open the door. "How'd it go?" Based on the sheriff's broad grin, my guess was pretty good.

"We're in luck," he said. "Found one of her strands of hair on his cloak. It's made of a polyester blend and all kinds of fibers stick to it. He really needs to wash it more regularly."

"Are you sure the hair is hers?" I asked. I pictured us tracking down Darth by mistake.

"Only one way to know for sure."

"Okay, let's go into the kitchen. It's where I do my best work."

Raoul made a noise that sounded like a garbled laugh and I shot him a dirty look.

"Um, Rose. I don't mean to judge, but why do you have an empty donut box on the floor? Can't you snack at the table like a normal witch?"

I scooped up the empty box and made a lame attempt to wipe away the powder. "This is Raoul's doing. He's been bringing lots of gifts home recently. He's suddenly very popular at the dump."

The sheriff lifted an eyebrow. "Is that so? You don't find that unusual?"

"Oh, I find it very unusual that he's popular."

My familiar's beady eyes turned to slits. *Don't make me go rabid.*

You go rabid in front of the sheriff and he'll have you put down. Now stay here and let the professionals work.

I disappeared into the kitchen with Sheriff Nash and hurried to the pantry. I rifled through Marley's herb collection and then retrieved the mortar and pestle from the cabinet.

91

The sheriff gave a nod of approval. "This looks real official Rose. All you need is a pointy hat and you're good to go."

I aimed my wand at him. "Watch it, werewolf, or you might find yourself on the wrong end of a spell."

He resisted the urge to smile. "Would that be by accident or on purpose?"

I growled before returning my attention to the locator spell. I tried to remember what Wren had taught me. He'd be pleased if I told him that I managed a successful spell outside of our lessons. Gold star for Ember!

The sheriff rubbed his hands together. "Anything I can do? I hate feeling idle."

"You're not idle," I said. "Just cool your heels for a second. As soon as I get the location, you're back in action."

He stuffed his hands in his pockets and fell silent. I busied myself with the spell, pulling out the ingredients and mashing them together. I lit the mixture on fire and then added the strand of hair. I pointed my wand at the mortar and said, "*Ostendo.*"

A familiar image flashed between us. A street lined with psychic services, including a sign for the Voice of the Gods.

"Seers Row," we said in unison.

I gulped for air. The spell had sucked the energy from me, probably a combination of being woefully out of practice and a long and busy day.

"Good work, Rose." The sheriff clapped me on the back.

I extinguished the fire and went to the sink to pour myself a glass of water. I noticed Bonkers hovering outside the window and opened it. The winged kitten perched on the ledge and meowed.

"I can't understand a word you're saying, but that makes you no less adorable," I said.

Bonkers wants to help, Raoul said.

I spun around. "When did you come in here? I told you to

stay out in the living room." I turned back to my daughter's familiar. "Do you want to help or is Timmy stuck in the well again?"

The winged kitten meowed softly.

"Sounds like a yes to me," the sheriff said.

"Great, Bonkers. You're on the team."

Why can't I be on the team? Raoul complained.

I glanced over my shoulder. "When we need someone to eat their way through a crime scene, you can be on the team." I faced the winged kitten. "We're looking for a brunette banshee. The spell says she's currently on Seers Row. Fly there now and try to keep tabs on her until we get there. Capisce?"

The winged kitten flew away without a backward glance.

"It's like having your own winged monkey," the sheriff said. "Except an adorable kitten." He rubbed his rugged jawline. "What does capisce mean? Is that witchy talk?"

"No, it's New Jersey Italian talk," I said. "At least that's where I picked it up. It means 'do you understand?' A lot of my friends' parents used to say it when we were growing up." I wagged a finger and did my best impression of Maria Gallo's mother. "Maria, this liquor cabinet better be in the same condition we left it when we get home from Uncle Vito's place in the Bahamas. Capisce?"

The sheriff chuckled. "It would've been fun to know you as a kid, I bet. Into all sorts of trouble."

"I wasn't bad, not really. I didn't want to cause my dad any grief. I figured he'd suffered enough, losing my mom. And Karl was in my life by then too."

"I guess having a baby when you're young is its own brand of trouble," the sheriff said. "Not that I'm saying Marley is any trouble."

"It's okay. I know what you mean," I said.

Aw, this exchange of deeply personal information is touching, but don't you have a suspect to apprehend?

I glared at the raccoon. *You're just jealous because I assigned Bonkers a task.*

Raoul climbed onto the countertop and started out the kitchen window. *I'm going back to the dump where I'm wanted.*

The problem was that the window was only partially open and his body got stuck.

"Looks like somebody's been overindulging in carbs," I said. "You might want to rethink all those gifts from your buddies." I raised the window another couple of inches and he wriggled through. I closed the window and locked it before turning back to the sheriff.

"Glad to see you locking your doors and windows," he said. "Until we catch this killer, we need to be on alert."

"Don't forget I've got the best home security in town." I pushed open the kitchen door and spotted my home security system snoring on the sofa in a tight ball. The Yorkshire terrier didn't bother to lift his head as the sheriff and I left the cottage.

"I see what you mean," the sheriff said wryly.

We drove to Seers Row and the sheriff parallel parked in the first available spot.

"You're much better at parking than Deputy Bolan," I said.

"That's because he can barely see over the dashboard," the sheriff said.

"Ooh, snap," I said. "I won't tell him you said that, unless he insults me and it's the first comeback I can think of. Then I'm throwing you under the bus."

The sheriff chuckled. "I can always count on you."

We stepped out of the car and I spotted Bonkers up ahead, hovering in front of a shop window. That was promising.

94

We passed Veronica's shop, the aforementioned Voice of the Gods, and I was relieved Nova wasn't in there. The psychic had a tendency to shriek and the thought of Nova's voice mixed in with that was enough to make me abandon our quest.

"Is she in that one, Bonkers?" I asked, as we approached the building.

The answer hit me before I even saw her. And by hit me, I mean assaulted my eardrums. The sheriff's hands flew to cover his ears.

"Are we sure she's not a dolphin shifter?" Sheriff Nash asked, wincing.

"Great balls of popcorn. It's worse than Janice," I said. I didn't think such a sound was possible.

"Who's Janice?" the sheriff asked.

"There's a television show in the human world called *Friends*," I said. "Janice was the ex-girlfriend of one of the main characters and her voice…" Elvis on a cracker, this was so much worse.

We pressed our faces against the window of a place called The Fourth Wall and peered at the scene inside. I spotted the backpack first, resting on the floor at the banshee's feet. The name *Nova* was emblazoned across the back in pink sparkly letters. The banshee stood at a cocktail table opposite a man in a…I squinted hard.

"Is he wearing a Deadpool costume?" I asked.

"I don't know who that is, but he's definitely in some kind of special outfit."

I snorted. "Psychic Deadpool. I love it."

"Looks like a tarot card reading," the sheriff said.

"Perfect. Let's see if he predicted our appearance." I pushed open the door and waved. "Hey, so sorry to interrupt. We were hoping for a reading."

"Welcome to The Fourth Wall, Sheriff Nash," Psychic

Deadpool said. "If you have a seat, I'll be with you in a moment."

We sat in two metal chairs by the window. I noticed a stack of magazines next to me and chose one entitled Psychic Interiors.

"Oh, this one has an article on pimped-out psychic offices," I whispered. I actually wanted to read it. I wondered whether there was a way I could sneak it into my bag, except it probably wasn't a good idea to commit theft in the company of the sheriff—or at all.

"What about this card?" Nova asked, ignoring our presence. "Does it mean my boyfriend will propose soon?"

Psychic Deadpool gazed at the card. "I'm not sure where you're getting that from. This is Death."

"Well, that's marriage for some paranormals, isn't it?" She tossed back her head and cackled in a way that made the hair on my arms stand straight.

"I understand that you're eager for that proposal as you've basically asked about it with every card you've chosen," the psychic said, "but I think the universe is trying to encourage you to make other plans."

Nova crossed her arms in a huff. "Does it say what the issue is? I mean, I do everything I can to please him. I cook and I hate to cook. I fake interest in the crap he likes to do. I wouldn't be here now if it weren't for the stupid tournament."

My gaze met the sheriff's. It sounded like Nova wasn't an actual participant. Come to think of it, Patton didn't mention that she had a phone, only that she was on the dock with them. She could have easily been sightseeing or killing time while she waited…or killing more than time.

The sheriff and I stayed silent and continued to listen. I flipped through the magazine and the sheriff stuck his nose in his phone.

Psychic Deadpool exhaled loudly. "As I've already mentioned five hundred times, the cards aren't a detailed journal of your life. I can't see specifics about your boyfriend, or whether he's seeing someone on the side, or whether he's noticed your new haircut." He mimicked her voice and I began to wonder if business was very good for him. While I agreed that she was something of a shrew, this didn't seem the right way to conduct business. His unprofessional behavior was probably the reason Veronica was popular. Plus, she had Jericho as her assistant. Who could compete with that dynamic duo?

"He notices my haircuts when I tell him I've had one." Nova slapped her hands on the table and shoved the cards aside. They fluttered to the floor in a scattered pile.

Psychic Deadpool threw up his hands. "What'd you do that for?"

"I didn't pay for bad news," she said.

"You didn't pay for anything yet," he said.

Nova turned to us. "Don't waste good coin on this phony. He doesn't get anything right."

The psychic adjusted his mask. "How can I help you? Will this be a double reading?"

"Not a reading. Just a few questions." The sheriff jerked his head toward Nova, who was now heading for the door.

"Sounds like a reading to me," Psychic Deadpool said.

I slipped out of the building behind her and left the sheriff to chat with Psychic Deadpool and see what he could find out about their spirited reading.

"That sounds like it sucked," I said, hurrying to fall in step beside her. "You should try Veronica. She's the best."

Nova stopped walking and looked at me, her rodent-like face scrunched in a ball. "That guy was minotaur shit. He kept saying my boyfriend and I have no future. He can't possibly know that. Those cards were useless."

Gee, who would've thought a guy in a Deadpool costume wouldn't provide the accurate information you were seeking?

"Sounds like you're having doubts about your relationship," I said.

Nova bristled. "I'm not. I'm just trying to keep busy this weekend. I thought a reading was a good idea. I tried the broomstick tour, but I almost vomited from the turns. Heights aren't my thing."

"You sound like my daughter," I said. "She's not a fan either, so I don't fly very often."

Nova looked me up and down. "You're a witch?"

"Yeah, I happen to love flying. I wish I had more time to do it."

"To each her own." She rocked back and forth on her heels. "Are you local? Any advice for activities? I've been here since Thursday and I'm verging on complete and total boredom."

"Are you here for the tournament?" I asked. "Why not play the game?"

She scoffed. "Are you kidding? Have you seen it? So dumb. I'm only here to keep my boyfriend from running off with some bimbo fairy while he's out of town."

"I don't know that I've seen many…bimbo fairies involved in the tournament. They're mostly guys." I paused for a beat. "So, I can offer sightseeing suggestions, but it would help to know which parts of town you've already seen." *Like Palmetto House, perhaps?*

Nova pursed her lips, thinking. "I did the broomstick tour, then I went to Mariner's Landing to throw bread-crumbs for the mermaids and selkies."

I wrinkled my nose. "They're not ducks."

Her smile was mean-spirited. "No, ducks are cuter."

"Where'd you start the morning?"

"Well, my boyfriend insisted on getting up at the crack of dawn to start the tournament." She rolled her eyes. "Who does that?"

"Pretty much every player here from the sound of it," I said.

"So dumb. Anyway, I slept late and had breakfast at a diner." She snapped her fingers. "Stake-n-Shake."

"By yourself?"

She scowled. "No need to rub it in."

"Any chance you've checked out the local architecture? Palmetto House is a beautiful historic building, if you like that sort of thing."

"That place sounds familiar," Nova said.

My pulse sped up. "It does?"

"I think we tried to stay there, but it was full by the time we got around to booking."

My spirits plummeted. "Yeah, it's at capacity because of the tournament." Well, not anymore. "Did you go to see it?"

"Why would I? I just told you we couldn't get in. I'm not going to make myself feel worse by checking it out."

Okay, time to try a different tack. "I've met some pretty cool guys this weekend. If you and your boyfriend are destined not to work out, maybe you'll meet someone else while you're here."

To my surprise, Nova actually looked interested. Her poor boyfriend. "Yeah? I've only seen losers so far like a dude in a dirty robe and a smelly werebear that asked me for directions. Where are the hot ones hanging out?"

"I met this guy Clark last night and he was..." I struggled to get the lie out. "...seriously smoking." I choked on the words.

"Clark doesn't sound like a smoking hot name," she said. "Is he a werewolf? They don't tend to like me. Not sure what puts them off."

"Gosh, I have no idea," I lied. "Clark's not a werewolf. He's a leprechaun."

She cackled and I was fairly certain I heard the sound of breaking glass in the distance. "Honey, I would never date a little green dude. I have something called standards."

"Have you met him?" I asked. "Because I think you might change your mind. He oozes confidence." Well, the only thing he oozed now was blood.

"I haven't met any leprechauns," Nova said. "If I did, I'd probably have ignored him anyway. If there's no point to meeting him, why would I bother?"

Nova was a real gem. "If you're looking for a good bar for later tonight, Elixir always draws a crowd." I wasn't about to direct her to the Whitethorn where I planned to be. I had standards too.

"Sounds like a cool place."

"It totally is. And if you're into activities, there's always unicorn riding or a simple game of tennis," I said.

Nova rubbed her wrists. "No way. After that broomstick ride, I need to give my opposable thumbs a rest."

"You held on that tightly, huh?" I asked.

"No, I suffer from horrible carpal tunnel in both my wrists," she said. "It's one reason I don't like texting. I can't hold a phone too long before I get sore. I don't think I'd do well with a tennis racquet either."

"I bet there's a potion for that," I said. Because there seemed to be a potion for every imaginable ailment.

"I have braces, but I didn't bring them. I don't like to wear them in front of my boyfriend," she said. "There's no way to make them sexy."

Nova seemed desperate to please someone by pretending to be someone she wasn't. As sad as it was, her relationship status wasn't my concern.

"I'm sure you can find a cute set of braces," I said diplomatically.

Nova scanned the street. "Which one is Veronica's? I think I'll give her a try. Maybe she'll have better news than that red pleather freak."

I pointed to Veronica's shop and silently apologized to the psychic and Jericho. "Good luck!"

The sheriff joined me on the curb as Nova disappeared into the building. "And?"

"And I don't think she did it," I said.

"She had an alibi?"

"No, she claims she was still asleep at the time of the murder, but I believe her," I said. "She had no idea who Clark was. She doesn't care about the tournament." All she cared about was herself. "She also suffers from carpal tunnel in both wrists. Didn't even want to consider lifting a tennis racquet."

The sheriff nodded. "That cast iron skillet is pretty heavy. She'd need to have lifted it high enough to whack him on the head."

"That was my thought," I said. "Not only would she have to hit him with it, but hard enough to kill him. I don't think she could do it."

"I trust your judgment, Rose, but we'll keep an eye on her, just to be safe."

"She won't be hard to find," I said. "I have a feeling she'll be stalking Seers Row until she gets the future she wants to hear."

The sheriff gave the shop a mournful look. "Hey, at least she has a future, which is more than I can say for Clark."

CHAPTER TEN

ON THE DRIVE back from Seers Row, Sheriff Nash was kind enough to swing by Haverford House so that I could collect Marley. I was surprised to see half a dozen players roaming the grounds in the dark. The only light came from their phone screens and a single light in the parlor room of Haverford House.

"Has it been like this the whole time?" I asked, as Marley scooted into the backseat.

"Pretty much," Marley said. "Hi, Sheriff."

He twisted to smile at her. "How's it going?"

"Good," she said. "I met so many interesting paranormals today. Artemis was in her element. She was even talking about throwing a ball."

"A ball?" I laughed. "How *Pride & Prejudice* of her."

"What's the matter, Rose? Don't want to powder your nose and string up a corset?"

"I'd rather hang out with Raoul at the dump," I said.

The sheriff dropped us off at the cottage and I thanked him for the ride.

"No need to thank me," he said. "You were a big help

today. I appreciate it."

It was one of the qualities I liked about Sheriff Granger Nash—he was always willing to express his appreciation and gratitude.

As we vacated the car, Marley's phone buzzed and she gasped excitedly. "Lucy wants to know if I can sleep over at her house tonight. Can I please, Mom?"

I unlocked the cottage door. "Are you sure you want to? You had a nightmare…"

"I won't have any nightmares. I promise."

PP3 attacked my legs with his tongue and his two front paws and I crouched down to pet him. "What about dinner? It's getting late and you haven't eaten."

"You don't have to worry about that," Marley said. "Artemis fed me about twenty finger sandwiches."

"And did you turn any of them into chocolate?" I asked pointedly.

"Only one," she mumbled.

"Did you play any of the game while you were there or did you serve tea and sandwiches the whole time?" I hooked the leash onto PP3's collar and guided him back to the door.

Her face brightened. "Oh, yeah. Everyone I met was super helpful. A gnome named Ted helped me defeat a dragon."

A gnome.

I halted in my tracks when it occurred to me that no one had spoken to Lewis yet. The sheriff had probably been too busy questioning other players and dealing with minor violations to track down the gnome. Now that we'd ruled out yet another suspect, I began to worry that Lewis was somehow involved in his friend's death.

"Can you check gardendelight's location?" I asked.

Marley frowned. "Is that Lewis?"

"Yes."

Marley clicked on the map. "Looks like he's at Fairy

Cove." She paused. "Since I helped you, can I sleep over at Lucy's?"

"Fine, if you're sure."

She jumped up and down and clapped. "I'm sure!"

"Then hurry up and pack a bag. I'll cancel Mrs. Babcock." I rushed the dog outside to pee, contemplating my next move. I was supposed to meet Alec at the Whitethorn anyway and Fairy Cove was on the way. I could drop off Marley and still have time to stop and talk to Lewis. If he'd been out playing all day, there was every chance he was clueless about Clark.

I didn't have a lot of time to freshen up for my night out with Alec, but I did my best. I managed to run a comb through my hair and brush my teeth. I changed into a silver top that sparkled when it caught the light. It was feminine without being downright girly.

I fed the dog and dropped off Marley. Before I left the driveway, I double-checked the gnome's location and saw that he'd moved on from Fairy Cove and was now in the vicinity of the Whitethorn. Perfect.

I debated whether to let Sheriff Nash know that I was about to interview Lewis, but decided against it. Alec was meeting me there and I didn't want to put either one in an awkward position.

The Whitethorn was overflowing with customers tonight. This was exactly what Florian and Aster had in mind when they decided to host the tournament. The ancient pub was not only a hot spot for the game, but it was a hot spot for evening socializing as well.

As I pushed my way through the crowd, Bittersteel, the resident parrot, caught sight of me. "Squawk! Pretty lady coming through. Make way for the witch!"

"Aye." Captain Yellowjacket's voice rang out. "Thar she blows."

I made my way over and rested my elbows on the counter. "You should really watch what you say," I told him. "That expression could be misconstrued." Especially in a room full of males.

"Business is booming," Captain Yellowjacket said. "Whatever magic your cousins worked to make this happen, I'm grateful for. A profitable weekend like this will get me through the down season."

"I'm glad it's working out for you," I said. "Unfortunately, it's not been so good for everyone."

He leaned across the bar and lowered his voice. "You're talking about the dead leprechaun, are you?"

Bittersteel perched on his captain's shoulder. "Squawk! Leprechaun down." A player within earshot squinted at his screen. "Are there leprechauns here? I haven't seen one. How many challenges are here?"

"We're talking about a real one," I said, resisting the urge to roll my eyes. Never in my New Jersey life could I have foreseen that I'd be rolling my eyes at someone for suggesting that a leprechaun was imaginary.

"No leprechaun challenges here, lad," Captain Yellowjacket confirmed. He poured me a pint and slid it across the counter. "It's been a steady stream of customers from the start of the tournament. Apparently, there is a nest of vampires to defeat, and if you manage that, then you get to battle an ogre."

"Ogre!" Bittersteel shrieked. Every head in the Whitethorn popped to attention.

"Another ogre?" someone yelled.

Captain Yellowjacket cupped his hands around his mouth. "Carry on, me hearties," he bellowed. "Nothing to see here." He glanced at the parrot on his shoulder. "You really need to pipe down. You're confusing them."

"I'm surprised they even know what day it is," I said. "This whole tournament is like Vegas. The game just goes on and on, regardless of the time of day or meals, showers, basic hygiene."

The vampire pirate chuckled. "There's definitely been a stench in here this weekend. I've been lighting scented candles to help mask the unpleasant odors."

Just then I glimpsed a familiar gnome in the crowd. I waved madly. "Lewis," I called.

The gnome was too intent on his screen to notice me. He held the phone in one hand and a large ale in the other.

"Friend of yours?" Captain Yellowjacket asked.

"He's staying at Palmetto House," I said.

The vampire pirate smiled, showing his fangs. "Ah, well I know this fellow is a friend of yours."

I turned to see the hottest vampire on the planet enter the Whitethorn and butterflies exploded in my stomach. Alec strode to the counter, parting the sea of paranormals like a vampire Moses.

"Did you finish your chapter?" I asked.

He greeted me with a kiss on the lips. "I did. I'm ready to rejoin reality."

"I'm glad to hear it," I said. "I'm just about to talk to Clark's friend. He's over in the corner." And was still engrossed in the game.

Alec gave the gnome a cursory glance. "The dead leprechaun?"

I nodded. "That's Lewis. He and Clark came together for the tournament."

"Don't let me get in the way of a good story," he said. "I'll order a drink and wait for you here."

"You're the best." I stood on my tiptoes and kissed him again. "I've missed you."

I maneuvered my way through the clusters of paranormals. It wasn't too hard. Most of them were standing perfectly still except for their fingers on their phone screens. I was secretly relieved that Marley didn't enjoy the game. I couldn't see her spending all her free time staring at a screen.

I tapped the gnome on the shoulder. "Hey, Lewis."

The gnome couldn't seem to drag his eyes away from the screen. "Hold on one sec. I'm about to kill this ogre. I've already failed twice and it keeps getting stronger." He continued to tap on his screen while muttering under his breath. Finally, he pumped his phone in the air and expressed victory.

"Congrats," I said. "I guess you got him this time."

"Darn right I did," Lewis said. "Nobody messes with gardendelight." He took a sip of ale. "Have you defeated the ogre yet? I can give you some tips now that I'm done." He seemed to notice that I was alone. "Where's your kid? I thought you two were playing together."

"Lewis," I said gently. "Do you know what happened to Clark?"

Lewis tugged his ear. "He's either ahead of me or behind me. I haven't seen him all day."

I wasn't sure how to break the news to him. These players were so invested in the tournament that they'd blocked out the murder of one of their own. That was some hardcore compartmentalization.

"He's definitely behind you," I said.

Lewis snorted. "I find that hard to believe. How can you be so sure?"

"Because he's dead."

Lewis blinked at me with his half-moon eyes. "You mean you killed a leprechaun in the game? Because they're like the easiest ones to kill."

I placed a hand on his shoulder. "Lewis, I'm sorry to be the one to tell you this, but Clark was found dead early this morning in the kitchen of Palmetto House."

The gnome shrank from my touch. "Is this some kind of sick joke? Because it's not very funny. I'm going to text him now." He tapped on his screen.

"He won't answer you," I said. "His phone is probably locked up in the sheriff's office right now."

Lewis blinked back tears. "Are you sure it was Clark? Maybe it was another leprechaun. It's easy to mix them up."

At least he had the decency not to ask about getting access to his friend's supplies in the game.

"I saw him myself," I said.

Lewis staggered back and threw up a hand to steady himself against the wall. "How? Why?"

"That's what we're trying to figure out," I said. "Did you see him at all this morning?"

Lewis rubbed his cheek, thinking. "Our rooms have an adjoining bathroom. It was locked when I went to brush my teeth this morning. I knocked and he said he'd be out in a minute."

"Do you remember what time that was?"

Lewis checked his phone records. "It had to be around five in the morning because I logged in right after I left the house."

"Did you have breakfast?"

"No, I rarely eat breakfast, and definitely not during tournaments. I get too anxious."

"You didn't plan to start the tournament together?" I asked.

"Clark's the opposite. He likes to play on a full stomach," the gnome said. "The smell of food would've been too much for me." He pinched the bridge of his nose. "Who would want to hurt Clark? I mean, I know he can be a pain and rub others the wrong way, but I can't imagine he would push someone so far that they'd want to kill him."

"He was the winner of the last tournament," I said. "Kind

of puts a target on his back. How about you? Have you ever won?"

He shook his head. "No, but it's cool. As long as I perform my best, I'm happy."

"You must be somewhat competitive though. Must make it hard to watch your friend win."

Lewis gulped down the rest of his ale. "Sure. We're all competitive to some degree. Otherwise, we wouldn't be participating. It's part of the lifestyle." He frowned. "You don't think I would actually hurt Clark over a game, do you? That's crazy."

"The sheriff's going to want to see your phone to confirm your story. In fact, I should probably let him know you're here." I took out my phone and opted to text Deputy Bolan instead.

Lewis stared into his empty glass. "I can't believe this is happening. Clark and I play this game together almost every day."

"Did anyone see you this morning between five and six?" I asked. "The sheriff is going to ask."

The gnome ran a finger around the rim of his glass, considering the question. "I saw a handful of shifters, a vampire, two elves." He swallowed hard. "I don't know any of their names though. I'm not even sure I spoke to any of them."

"Where did you see them?" I asked. "A hot spot?"

Lewis set his empty glass on a passing tray. "No, just out and about after I left Palmetto House. Everyone seemed to be headed in a different direction."

"Is there anyone you can think of that we should talk to? Anybody with a grudge against Clark aside from the were-bear from last night?"

"You talked to him already?" Lewis asked. "I was going to tell you about that."

"Buck's been cleared."

Lewis pursed his lips. "Anybody who pays attention knows Clark was someone to keep an eye on." His eyes sparked with an idea. "You should talk to Sara."

"Who's Sara?"

He made a face of contempt. "She's a troll with a mouth as big as her feet. She shows up at all the tournaments, always talking smack but never delivering. Don't think she's ever even placed, yet she doesn't shut up about being successful."

"Did she have a run-in with Clark?"

"Not sure about here, but they argued at the last tournament in River Run where Clark won. I'm not exaggerating when I tell you she was a very sore loser."

That sounded like a promising lead. "Have you seen Sara today?"

He made a dismissive sound. "No way. She'd have to be much further along in the game to be anywhere I am. You'll probably find her still trying to sharpen her stake to kill the first vampire. You need to acquire a special knife to do the sharpening."

"Do you remember where you did that?"

"I think it was near the big fountain with the statues in town. I only remember because some of the water splashed onto my screen and I had to dab at it with the bottom of my shirt." He shook his head slowly. "It could have been a catastrophe."

Yes, that would have been the real catastrophe. Never mind the murdered leprechaun. "Any idea what her user name is?"

Lewis laughed. "I do, as a matter of fact. We're not friends on the game, but I happen to know she goes by ogreeasy."

"Is that an egg yolk?" I couldn't help myself.

Lewis looked at me like I had two heads. "I think it's supposed to mean she kills ogres easily."

Time to retreat before I made a bigger fool of myself.

"Thanks for your help, Lewis." I cast a glance over my shoulder to see the deputy entering the Whitethorn. Perfect timing. "Here comes Deputy Bolan now. When he's done looking at your phone, do you want a lift back to Palmetto House? I'm heading in that direction."

He gave me a blank look. "Why would I do that? I killed the ogre. I'm going to move on to the next achievement. If I'm tired after that, then I'll go to bed."

I balked. "You're going to continue the game?"

Lewis's expression turned solemn. "It's what Clark would have wanted."

Oddly enough, I agreed with him. "Good luck," I said. I gestured to Deputy Bolan and inclined my head toward Lewis. The leprechaun seemed to get the idea, so I started back toward Alec. He was already finished with his drink.

"Not the killer, I take it?" the vampire asked.

I shook my head. "I don't think so. He did give me another lead though. I need to find a troll called Sara."

Alec smiled, revealing his impressive fangs. "Care to make a date of it?"

I laughed. "It's a little macabre to make a date of chasing down a murder suspect, don't you think?"

Alec pushed the empty glass across the counter. "I don't mind what we do, as long as we do it together."

"I love the sentiment, but it's late. I'm going to leave Sara for tomorrow and focus on you tonight." I opened the game on my phone and added ogreeasy as a friend so that I could track her down more easily. Hopefully, she'd accept the request by the time I wanted to find her.

He clasped my hands in his. "I have a better suggestion. Why don't you leave Sara for the sheriff to question?"

"Because he and Deputy Bolan are up to their eyeballs in work thanks to the tournament," I said. "They can use the help and I'm much better at asking questions than I'd be at handling traffic violations." Not to mention I could get away with asking questions as a reporter. It would be much harder to justify pulling over speeding cars, although it might be fun for an afternoon.

Alec leaned his forehead against mine. "It would be nice to spend time together tomorrow."

"Listen, you have no room to talk. You've been holed up with your manuscript for ages when you could've been spending time with me."

He cupped the back of my head. "I'm with you now, so let's make the best of it."

"If we're going to make the best of it, then I suggest we go back to the cottage. Marley's sleeping at a friend's house tonight. We can even sleep in. Together."

His lips curved into a seductive smile, revealing his impressive fangs. "Then by all means, Ms. Rose. Lead the way."

CHAPTER ELEVEN

As MUCH AS I hated leaving the warmth of Alec and the bed, I wanted to get a jump on the day. Sara was likely roaming the town already, killing whatever obstacles the game put in front of her—though not very well, according to Lewis.

Alec reached for me as I rolled to the edge of the bed. "I thought we were sleeping in."

"We did. It's seven."

"That's hardly a lie-in."

"It is when you have an old dog and a school-aged daughter."

He slid across the bed and tried to urge me back into bed. "Your suspect is probably still snoring."

"Then you haven't been paying attention. These players don't mess around." I swung my legs over the side of the bed and stretched. "Are you coming to Thornhold for dinner tonight? Aunt Hyacinth specifically invited you because Philip Muldoon will be there. I think she wants as many buffers as possible."

"I'm afraid I'll have to pass," he said. "If I spend most of the day with you, my book will require my attention this evening."

"That book is like your mistress."

He smiled. "Ember, are you jealous of a book?"

"No, I'm jealous of the attention your book gets compared with me."

He kissed my shoulder. "I'm sorry. I'll do better. It's just that I've been battling with the murky middle and finally had a breakthrough."

I craned my neck to look at him. "I know. You don't have to explain. It's not like I have nothing else to do. I just like spending time with you." I shifted to face him. "That thing you said about your therapy appointment…When you asked if you were a mistake."

His smile melted away. "We needn't speak of it. A mere slip of the tongue."

"Just so we're clear—you could never be a mistake, Alec."

He entwined his fingers with mine. "Then come back to bed and prove it."

"Ha! Manipulation will get you nowhere."

"Very well then." He peeled back the sheet and rose to his feet. "I'll cook breakfast, shall I?"

"Watch out for any gifts Raoul might have snuck into the house during the night. You don't want to step on a jelly donut."

"Indeed."

I showered and dressed and was pleased to inhale the aroma of bacon and eggs on my way downstairs. Nope, the vampire was definitely not a mistake.

Raoul was in the kitchen staring longingly at the plates on the table. Alec seemed obvious to the raccoon. He gazed out the window as he sipped his coffee, probably lost in a world of his own creation.

"One piece, Raoul, but that's it," I said.

The raccoon swiped a strip of bacon from my plate and devoured it. *Where's the kid?*

She stayed overnight at a friend's.

So this fangaroo could hop into your pouch?

I joined Alec at the table and turned my back to Raoul. *Don't you have gifts to receive down at the dump from your newfound admirers?*

Raoul scampered to the kitchen door. *You're right. I bet I get more than a measly scrap of bacon too.*

Ungrateful trash panda. I didn't have to share at all.

Sure you did. It's one of the first provisions of the Familiar Pact.

"Would you like tea or coffee?" Alec asked.

"Right now I want to inhale my food, but thanks."

Raoul pushed open the door and let it slam shut behind him.

"Someone's in a mood," Alec said.

"I don't know why. He's being treated like the king of the dump lately. You'd think he'd be ecstatic." I shoveled eggs into my mouth. "Breakfast is delicious. Thank you."

"The most important meal of the day."

I gnawed on a strip of bacon as I checked the game on my phone. I was pleased to see that Sara had accepted my friend request. "Want to come with me to talk to Sara? You said we could make a date of it."

He smiled behind his coffee mug. "And I believe you said that was macabre."

"Maybe you could flash your fangs and intimidate her into spilling the beans," I said.

"And if she's innocent? What will I have accomplished then?"

I wagged a piece of bacon at him. "Good point. Maybe just stand behind me and look hot." I crunched the bacon.

"Perhaps I could be helpful in some other capacity."

115

"Nope. Just smolder behind me. That's all I need." My phone lit up with a text. "Marley wants me to pick her up in an hour." If I hustled, I'd have just enough time to track down Sara first. "Would you mind taking the dog for a quick walk? I need to get moving."

Alec swallowed a mouthful of coffee. "I did say I wanted to be helpful."

I laughed. "And now you're regretting it."

"Care to rendezvous for lunch?"

I pushed back my chair. "Raincheck. I'll have Marley and I also want to look through the information I got from the archives about Ivy." I'd been so focused on Clark's murder that I'd barely given the list a second glance.

His brow lifted. "Anything illuminating?"

"Not sure yet. It's possible, but I don't want to get my hopes up." I cleared our plates from the table and deposited them in the sink. "Stay as long as you like. PP3 seems used to you now."

"Raoul seems resentful."

"Raoul resents anyone that isn't feeding him." On my way to the door, I stopped to give Alec a goodbye kiss. "I think I'll ride the broomstick you bought me."

"What about Marley? She won't want to ride home with you on it, will she?"

"You know what? She has to learn as part of the curriculum at the Black Cloak Academy. She might as well sneak in a little practice with her mother. It's not far from Lucy's house, so she won't have to ride very long." And I'd fly lower to the ground so as not to exacerbate her anxiety.

I left the kitchen and looked around the cottage for my broomstick. I didn't get to fly as often as I liked, but now seemed like the perfect time to hop on board. The dog lifted his tired head from his front paws.

"Do you know where my broomstick is?" I asked.

PP3 seemed to understand my question because he jumped down and trotted to the coat closet where he sniffed along the crack between the door and the floor. I opened the door and saw the broomstick hanging on a hook like a coat.

"Clever dog," I said, and bent down to pat the Yorkie's head.

He barked in acknowledgement and I grabbed my purse before heading outside. According to the game map, Sara was at Muse Fountain just as Lewis predicted. It seemed she was struggling to complete the challenge.

I straddled the broomstick and prepared for takeoff. Flying was very much like riding a bike. Actually, it was even easier because there was no need to pedal. I only needed to not plummet hundreds of feet to the earth and die a painful death. Okay, maybe not easier.

I launched into the air and felt a rush of excitement as the wind blasted through my hair. Flying truly was an exhilarating experience. There was also the added bonus that I was good at it. There weren't too many things I could say that about with confidence.

I spotted the troll from the air and landed on the opposite side of Muse Fountain. With my broom in hand, I waltzed around the perimeter of the fountain to where Sara was seated with her back against the base of the fountain. At first I thought she was engrossed in the game until I saw her pull out a handkerchief and blow her nose. It was only then that I realized she was crying.

"Sara?" I approached with caution because Sara was a rather large troll. Even seated on the ground she reached my chest.

The troll looked up at me with red-rimmed eyes. Water marks streaked her cheeks and the end of her wide nose looked sore and angry. "What do you want?" she snapped.

"I'm sorry to interrupt. My name is Ember Rose and I'm a

reporter for the local paper. I was hoping to ask you a few questions about the tournament."

She jerked her phone toward me. "Do I look like I can answer questions? I'm stuck on this challenge and I can't level up until I complete it. It's already Sunday and I'm losing valuable time." Her face grew flushed.

"Unfortunately, my questions are more pressing than your challenge. I need to ask you about Clark."

She rubbed her eye. "Who's Clark?"

I could tell from her expression that she knew exactly who Clark was. "Pro tip—don't ever try to play poker. You'll lose big time."

Sara hobbled to her feet. "Watch what you say, lady. I don't lose, okay? I might be slow to win, but I do not lose."

I folded my arms. "How long have you been trying to acquire the knife?"

Her guilty glance told me what I needed to know. "There's a glitch," she said. "I should have gotten that knife yesterday. It's the game's fault."

Right. "I'm surprised there aren't more players congregated here if it's a glitch. How are the other players managing to get past it?"

"Cheaters," she said heatedly. "Some of the others cheat and gang up on players like me."

"Gang up how?"

She scrunched her face in a show of frustration. "They help each other, but they don't help me."

"Why don't we talk about Clark?"

"Sure, why not? He's one of them. His little group always helps each other and they blow right past me like I don't exist."

"Did that happen today?" I asked.

"Of course. Every tournament." She straightened her shoulders. "But I don't need them. I can win on my own."

It didn't seem likely. "Are you telling me you saw Clark yesterday or today?"

"I'm sure he was in that group that I passed at Haverford House yesterday."

"What time was that?" I asked.

"Maybe noon."

Either Sara was lying because she knew better or she really didn't know about Clark. I found it incredible that these players were so enthralled by the game that they blocked out everything else.

"Sara, you couldn't have seen Clark at noon yesterday."

Her eyes narrowed. "Now you're telling me I'm wrong about what I saw with my own two eyes? You're as bad as the rest of them."

Sara seemed to suffer from a victim complex. That explained her failure to succeed. She probably spent most of her time getting in her own way.

"You can't have seen Clark at noon yesterday because he'd already been dead for about six hours."

Sara jutted out her sizable chin. "Then I must've seen his ghost."

Wow. The denial was strong in this troll. "Other than his ghost, when did you last see Clark?"

Sara perched on the edge of the fountain. Half her trousers hung over the edge and grazed the water, but she didn't seem to notice.

"Friday, on the way to my B&B," she said. "I saw him and his buddy at that coffee shop, the Caffeinated Cauldron."

"Did you stop to talk to them?"

Her nostrils flared. "Why would I? They don't like to talk to me because they know I'm going to win and they're jealous."

"How many of these tournaments have you won?"

She shifted her bottom slightly. "I would win all of them,

except for these glitches. They probably did something to my phone when I was in the coffee shop. That must be why I can't get the knife."

"Maybe you could have someone take a look at your phone and make sure it's functioning properly," I said, knowing perfectly well that her phone hadn't been tampered with. I'd met people like Sara back in New Jersey, especially in my old line of work. Professional victims that loved to blame everyone else for their problems and never take responsibility for their own behavior. When you repossess cars for a living, you're bound to encounter a lot of these people.

"I had an elf look at it earlier—they're usually good at tinkering—but he said he couldn't find anything wrong with mine." She scowled. "I think he was friends with Clark and that crew. He probably wants one of them to win."

"I doubt everyone wants Clark to win," I said, unable to keep my mouth shut. "Since he won the last one, I'm sure they'd rather someone else manage it this time around."

Sara snapped her sausage fingers. "That reminds me—when I was in the coffee shop, I saw Clark get into an argument with a werewolf."

"Another player?"

"I think so," she said. "Someone called him Benny. He was wearing a fedora, which looked really stupid."

A werewolf in a fedora shouldn't be too difficult to locate. "Do you know what they were arguing about?"

"No, I missed that part, but Clark got all red-faced, which made him look like one of those tiny Christmas trees." She smiled at the memory.

"Thanks, Sara. That's helpful." I shot off a quick text to the sheriff to track down a fedora-wearing werewolf named Benny.

"Well, yeah. Of course it is. I'm not like those other guys.

A rising tide lifts all boats, except the one I'm in. That one, they'd rather torpedo."

Wow. She couldn't even accept a gracious comment without playing the victim card. "Maybe you could ask someone to help you get the knife," I said.

"I don't need help," she snapped. "I do it all on my own. That's why they can't stand me."

Yes, that's why.

As she turned away from me, I spotted a wet patch across her bottom. If this had been anyone else, I probably would've let them know and performed a quick drying spell.

"Have a good day, Sara," I said cheerfully.

"Don't tell me what to do," the troll snarled. She gave me the finger and kept walking.

CHAPTER TWELVE

MARLEY WASN'T THRILLED when I arrived at her friend's house on a broomstick, but, to her credit, she rode home without complaint. She did, however, leave indentation marks on my waist.

"Have you found the killer yet?" Marley asked, once we were safely on the ground.

"Not yet. Still working on it." I unlocked the cottage door with a twinge of sadness, knowing that Alec would be gone. Maybe I should've stayed in bed with him instead of chasing after a dead end. Then again, there was no way to know Sara was a dead end without speaking to her—and she did provide me with another lead. A sigh escaped my lips. I guess I was as guilty of immersing myself in a project as Alec. Then again, he was using work to avoid emotions and self-reflection. I was…What was my excuse?

"What's the matter, Mom?"

"I'm disappointed that Clark's killer is still out there." I managed a smile. "How was your sleepover?"

"Great. We stayed up until past midnight." She dropped

her bag and raced to the sofa to pet the dog. PP3 licked her hand like it was made of chicken and peanut butter.

"So that means an early bedtime tonight."

She pulled a face. "We have dinner at Aunt Hyacinth's though. That runs late."

"Not tonight it won't. I have too much to do." I'd been pushing aside everything except the investigation. I needed to regroup.

"That reminds me. I still have homework to finish."

I thought about Ivy's list of words on my phone. "Why don't we do homework together?"

Marley beamed as though I'd offered her a brownie sundae with extra whipped cream. Only my child would be elated to tackle homework in tandem with her mother.

"I'll get my backpack." She ran upstairs and returned in record time. "What are you working on?"

I sat on the sofa and opened the notes app on my phone where I'd typed Ivy's seemingly random words. "I was able to get access to information about Ivy's problems with the coven."

Marley's mouth formed a circle. "Why didn't you tell me?"

"I've been too busy to give it any attention." I studied the unfamiliar words. "The coven seemed to think her magic was driving her mad."

"Is that why they took it away?"

I nodded. "There was a trial where they interrogated her. Ivy's answers were lucid, but she would sprinkle in foreign words that seemed to have no place in the sentence."

Marley joined me on the sofa and peered at the list. "I know that word. Shamash means sun."

I looked at her agape. "How?" I wasn't sure why I was surprised. Marley's knowledge far exceeded my own when it came to anything remotely academic.

Marley pressed her lips together, deep in thought. "It was

a spell we did in class to help plants grow. The teacher said it was an ancient spell and that's why the key words were in ancient Sumerian instead of Latin."

My eyes widened. "You think these words are ancient Sumerian?"

She leaned over my shoulder and examined the other words. "I think so."

"Are you sure?"

"Yes! I recognize these. They're the elements." She tapped the screen. "Were they written in all capital letters?"

"No."

"That's probably because the coven scribe didn't realize what she was saying. That's why they assumed they were nonsense." She pointed. "Kia is earth, but you'd spell it K-I-A. Ag should be A-G and it means fire."

"I guess they could still be the ramblings of a madwoman," I said.

"No, I don't think so." Her face was aglow. Nothing seemed to energize my daughter more than knowledge. "Mom, I think it's an incantation."

My pulse sped up. "What makes you think that?"

"These aren't random words. You said they were sprinkled throughout her answers?"

"Yes, KIA was in the middle of one sentence. AG was in the middle of another answer. They weren't together."

"Well, they're connected. They make sense when read together."

My whole body tingled. I knew Ivy wasn't crazy—that there'd been a rhyme or reason for the words. I'd felt it in my bones.

Marley's gaze met mine. "Why do you think she did that?"

"I think it might be the spell she created to break the ward on the Book of Shadows."

Marley stared at the words in awe. "Why would she do that?"

"Maybe she knew that it was a way of hiding the incantation that would last beyond her lifetime or maybe she was worried that they'd mess with her memory and she'd forget." My mind was spinning with possibilities. "Or maybe she hid it for someone in particular. It would've had to be someone in the coven with access to the transcript though." Unless the information hadn't always been as restricted as it was now.

Marley blinked. "The incantation might have been meant for someone she wanted to be the gatekeeper of her Book of Shadows?"

"Not just of the book," I said, my heart racing. "Of her magic." And considerable power.

Marley's brow wrinkled. "Something must've happened then because they never used it, not if the Book of Shadows is still locked."

"Unless they weren't meant to use it. Only to have the metaphorical key in case of emergency," I said.

Marley clapped her hands. "Mom, this is so exciting! It might be the answer we've been looking for."

"There's only one way to know if I'm right."

Marley bolted from the sofa and started toward the staircase.

"Where are you going?" I asked.

"You're going to need the wand," she said. "I think we should have the grimoire here too, just in case."

"We?" I echoed. "Marley, I don't think you should be involved. If the magic is as powerful as it seems, then I don't want you within range of it."

Marley lifted her chin in defiance. "Aunt Hyacinth gave the wand and the grimoire to me. She must think I can handle it."

"Sweetheart, Ivy couldn't handle it and she was a grown

witch. I'd prefer to be cautious," I said. "If I manage to open the book and everything seems kosher, then I'll reconsider."

My response seemed to satisfy her. She hurried upstairs to retrieve the items and returned before I had a chance to sneak a cookie from my secret stash in the kitchen. She set the wand and grimoire on the coffee table and looked at me expectantly.

"I think you should go to Thornhold," I said. "No, wait. Go to Florian's man cave." I didn't want Aunt Hyacinth to know what we were doing.

"He's probably busy with tournament stuff," Marley said.

"Then go ride Firefly," I suggested. The unicorn would likely be pleased to get out of the stables for a bit.

"That'll take too long," Marley said. "I don't think you'll be more than half an hour."

I patted her arm. "That's optimistic of you."

"You have all the items plus the spell," she said. "If you can't do it now, then I don't think you'll ever be able to manage it."

"Okay, now I feel less supported," I said. "Why don't you take PP3 and play in the woods? I'll text you when it's safe to come back."

Marley scrunched her face, seeming to debate whether she should put up more of a fight. In the end, she relented. "Fine."

I nudged her toward the door, eager to get started. "Don't forget a bag."

She grimaced. "Do you think he needs to poop?"

"No, but if you forget the bag, he definitely will. That's how it works."

She stuffed a green bag into her pocket and grabbed the leash. At the sight of the leash, PP3 came barreling toward her. Suddenly, he was a spry puppy again, ready to chew on furniture and run off with my sneakers. The leash was its own form of magic.

"Don't let him in the pond," I said. "I don't want to smell wet dog all night."

Marley snatched her phone from the dining table and slid it into her back pocket. "If I don't hear from you in twenty minutes, I'm coming back!"

"Deal."

"Good luck," Marley called. She shut the door behind her and I took a deep breath. It was showtime.

I studied the three items on the coffee table. The grimoire didn't seem necessary for this experiment, so I moved it to the chair. I wanted to minimize distractions. As I sat back on the sofa, I saw something I hadn't noticed before. Thanks to the position of the wand on the coffee table and its proximity to the Book of Shadows, I realized that the bottom of the wand was about the same size and shape as a hole on the cover of the book. I pulled the book onto my lap and fit the wide end of the wand into the space, like a key into a lock.

It was a perfect fit.

Nothing happened, of course, probably because I hadn't performed the incantation. I was more convinced than ever that the seemingly random words in the transcript were deliberately placed. Ivy Rose wasn't driven mad by magic— she was crazy like a fox. I reviewed the words one more time and released an anxious breath. Placing both hands on the wand, I held it in place as I recited each word, careful to enunciate each letter. Marley had told me there was no silent syllables in Sumerian and that each letter was sounded out. One wrong pronunciation and I could trigger the protective ward. I'd made it halfway through the list when the wand began to tremble. It was either resistance or progress.

Sweet baby Elvis, I wish I knew which one it was.

I kept going. The book began to glow with an orange

light, as though it were about to combust. The wand shook with the force of a jackhammer and I was glad to already have two hands on it.

I uttered the final word—PETA. A powerful force tossed me up and over the back of the sofa. I missed the dining table and landed hard against the wall. When I recovered my senses, I realized my hands were empty. Despite a throbbing head, I crawled back to the sofa to find the Book of Shadows. The wand was on the floor and the book was still on the sofa, minus the orange glow. I climbed back onto the sofa and hesitantly tried to lift the cover.

The book opened.

I whooped so loudly I was sure that Aunt Hyacinth probably heard me in Thornhold. I started paging through the book. Some of the entries seemed to be written in Sumerian. The pages reminded me of a scrapbook with scraps of material mixed in with images and handwritten entries. This would be a lot to process. Maybe I'd ask Delphine for help, although I'd have to swear her to secrecy. I didn't want word of this book leaking out. If the enormity of Ivy's power was to be believed, it was too dangerous.

"Mom?" Marley entered the cottage a few minutes later with a worn-out PP3.

I gave her a giddy smile and held up the open book to show her. "I did it!"

Marley continued to stare at me with her mouth open. "Mom…"

"Oh, sorry. *We* did it. I didn't mean to steal your thunder, sweetheart."

"It's not that," she said. "Have you looked in a mirror since you opened the book?"

"Why would I?" I was vain, but I wasn't so vain that I needed to give my reflection a victorious wink.

Marley bit her lip. "Did the book do anything…strange when you opened it?"

"It exploded and blew me across the room, if that's what you mean."

She nodded. "Okay, that explains it."

Now I had to look. I opened the mirror app on my phone and screamed at my reflection. The ends of my hair were singed and pieces were sticking straight up as though I'd been electrocuted. There was also a coating of black dust on my face.

"You can tell how excited I was because I didn't sense this at all." I put the phone on the coffee table.

"Are you sure you're not hurt?" She joined me on the sofa, leaving a comfortable gap between us.

"My head hurts and I'm sure the rest of me will be sore later. I'm not limber enough to take a tumble like that and not pull a muscle or two." I didn't care about aches and pains right now though. I had opened Ivy's Book of Shadows and that was all that mattered.

Now that Marley was reassured about my condition, she turned her focus to the open book. "I can't believe it. What's it like?"

"It's a little difficult to understand at times because of the unfamiliar words and phrases," I admitted. "It's also a disjointed story. It's not in chronological order so it's hard to follow. I'll need to try to create my own timeline so I can piece it all together."

Marley leaned over for a better view. "I can help with that. I'm good at timelines. I've done them at school in history class. There are even software programs that can sort out information by date."

"Maybe another time," I said. Truth be told, the quick glimpses I got of Ivy's memories in English were distressing. If I was understanding the entries correctly, it seemed that she was under constant scrutiny and criticism by the rest of the coven. They were particularly unhappy when she was chosen as High Priestess. There had been a ceremony where the name of the next High Priestess was whispered by the wind. Apparently, everyone heard Ivy's name during that ceremony, yet there was still a disagreement as to whether to appoint her. Her authority was controversial from the very beginning. It was surprising, given the amount of respect to descendants of the One True Witch, but Ivy clearly had her detractors early on. Maybe because they were uncomfortable with her potential. Although I got the sense that powerful women were more acceptable in a coven than they would have been in the human world during that period, Ivy's advanced level might have been a bridge too far.

"Look what else I found." I turned back a few pages and showed Marley an image I had spotted.

"It's a hive," she said, "like the one we summoned when we tried to summon Ivy's spirit."

"I thought you'd remember," I said with satisfaction.

The image depicted a bee with a tiny crown hovering outside the busy and active hive. I noticed that the queen bee was facing the hive rather than away from it, as though she wanted back in. Ivy had been cast out and stripped of her magic, so it made sense that she would have wanted to be reinstated, to be part of the coven again. I felt a rush of sympathy for her. Ivy must've felt like she'd been forced to change at her very core. I didn't envy her.

"What now?" Marley asked.

"We take our time," I said. "We keep this between us for now. Don't tell anyone, not even Florian." I noticed her downturned expression. "What's wrong?"

"I thought it would be overflowing with magic or something," Marley said. "Ivy went to such great lengths to hide it and lock it, but it just seems like an ordinary book."

I placed my hands on the cover and felt the power radiating from inside. There was no way this was an ordinary book, but I was happy to let Marley believe that until I knew more. I still didn't want to risk endangering her. For all we knew, simply having the Book of Shadows unlocked in the cottage would create issues we never anticipated. I couldn't be too careful.

"I'll make it my special research project," I said. "Until I have more information, though, I don't want you to touch it."

Marley laughed. "Come on, Mom. Don't you think you're being paranoid?"

I hugged the book to my chest. "Like you said, Ivy went to great lengths. Let's trust her judgment until we have a reason not to."

Her head bobbed up and down. "You're right. This is so cool. I can't believe we have access to all her stuff now."

"We should probably get cleaned up for dinner," I said. "You know Aunt Hyacinth will want us all glamorous to impress Philip."

"But he won't be fooled. He's already met us."

I laughed. "Good point."

Marley pointed at my head. "I think you need a shower. Even without a family dinner, you don't want anyone to see you like this."

"Fair enough." I contemplated the book. "We need to find a good hiding place for this now that it's open. Somewhere no one would find it."

"The oven," Marley said without hesitation. "You don't use it and no one else would think of looking there."

I cast a sidelong glance at her. "I want to be insulted, and yet I'm forced to admit it's a great idea." I scooped up the Book of Shadows and Marley reclaimed the wand.

"I swear it feels different now," Marley said. "I think it's humming."

"That's probably your imagination," I said. "It's the power of suggestion, now that you know the ward has been broken, you're on the lookout for signs of powerful magic."

Marley smiled. "Now you sound like me."

"Just what this cottage needs—two clever witches." I carried the book into the kitchen and placed it in the oven. Then I conjured a quick spell to lock down the oven so that no one could turn it on or open the door. There was always a chance that Raoul could decide to warm a box of pizza in the oven. As I headed upstairs to shower, I felt a faint tingle in my hands and brushed them on my top. The sensation reminded me of static electricity but without the shock. Probably residual magic from the book. Whatever it was, I had to get rid of it by dinner. If there was magic in the air, I had no doubt Aunt Hyacinth would sniff it out and I wasn't remotely ready to share the news—not until I knew more about what happened to Ivy and why.

CHAPTER THIRTEEN

"PHILIP, WELCOME BACK TO THORNHOLD." Aunt Hyacinth sashayed into the foyer, her purple kaftan swirling around her ankles. She clasped Philip's hands and kissed each cheek, an unusually affectionate greeting for the reserved witch.

Marley tapped my arm. "I thought she didn't like him," she whispered.

"She doesn't, but she's not about to show bad manners," I said.

"That wouldn't stop you," Marley whispered again.

"That's because I grew up in New Jersey. Now shush."

Philip stepped back to admire her. "You look as lovely as I remember."

"I bet that's a clever way of saying not lovely at all," Marley said under her breath.

I elbowed her to be quiet. The last thing I needed was to draw Aunt Hyacinth's attention. My hands were still tingling mildly from the Book of Shadows explosion, so I was hoping to avoid eye contact—or any contact—with my aunt.

He squinted at the design on her kaftan. "Are those kittens with wings?"

Aunt Hyacinth gave him a sour look. "Of course. What else would they be?" She inclined her head toward us. "I had this one made in honor of Marley's familiar. You know she recently came into her magic."

"Yes, I heard the good news." He turned and winked at us. "Sounds like it was a real nail-biter."

"Can I offer you an aperitif?" my aunt asked.

"Nothing for me, thanks," Philip said. "I avoid alcohol during tournaments. I'd rather not compromise my reflexes." His gaze traveled over the decor and furnishings. "This place looks the same as I remember. My cousin had excellent taste."

Aunt Hyacinth's smile tightened and I knew she was fighting the urge to take credit for the selections. Through clenched teeth, she said, "He married me, didn't he?"

"Where's everyone else?" I asked, inching closer to break the tension. "Usually, we're the last ones to show up."

"Yes, punctuality isn't one of your strengths, is it?" my aunt said.

"Birds of a feather," Philip said, smiling. "I'm not a big fan of time either."

Aunt Hyacinth bristled. "It isn't something you choose to support or not support. That's like saying you're not a fan of the earth being round."

Marley raised a finger. "There are people who believe that…"

"They're not called people, darling. They're called morons." Aunt Hyacinth turned on her heel and waltzed into the dining room.

Philip chuckled. "She hasn't changed a bit."

"You don't seem to mind," I said.

He seemed surprised. "What's to mind? I like a little personality to shake things up. It was always obvious to me what my cousin saw in her."

"She only started dating again recently," Marley volunteered. "She's been alone all this time."

Philip's brow wrinkled. "Is that so? I hadn't realized. Who's the lucky wizard?"

"Why do you assume he's a wizard?" Marley asked.

Philip smiled. "Because we're talking about Hyacinth Rose-Muldoon. She wouldn't dream of dating outside the coven."

I decided not to share the details of my aunt's recent dating adventures. "His name is Craig and he's very nice," I said.

"Will he be dining with us this evening?" Philip asked.

"I don't think so," I said. "She probably thought it would be in bad taste."

"Oh, she's been a widow been long enough," Philip said. "She should know I want her to be happy."

We trailed into the dining room and Philip took my usual seat adjacent to my aunt. I was relieved to have someone between us for a change—a nice buffer.

"It's a shame Alec's too busy to join us," Aunt Hyacinth said.

I pulled out the chair beside Philip. "He said he's sorry to miss it."

The rest of the family streamed into the room and Philip stood to greet everyone. The only ones he hadn't seen yet were Aster's husband Sterling and their twin boys, Aspen and Ackley.

"Hey, I have that shirt," Aspen said. The little boy pointed at Philip's T-shirt with the picture of a seal saying 'I approve.'

"Yes, but you were smart enough not to wear it to Sunday dinner," Aunt Hyacinth said coolly.

"Mom told me no," Aspen said.

"So you can wear flying cats on your muumuu, but I can't have an adorable seal?" Philip asked.

"My look is age appropriate, whereas your taste in clothes hasn't changed in the past two decades," my aunt said.

"No need to fix what isn't broken," Philip replied cheerfully. Nothing seemed to rattle this wizard. He was definitely growing on me.

"Ember, you look remarkably pretty this evening," my aunt said. "Did you change your hair?"

I nearly fell off my chair. Did my aunt really just pay me a backhanded compliment? I mean, the backhand part was a given, it was the compliment that threw me for a loop.

"I washed it," I said.

Philip wiped his mouth with a cloth napkin, smothering a laugh.

Simon swooped into the room and served the drinks. I watched in surprise as Marley aimed her wand at her glass and changed her white milk into chocolate milk.

"No wands at the table," I said, trying to be quiet but firm. If the twins caught sight of chocolate milk, a riot was going to erupt.

"Philip has a phone," Marley said. "Why can't I have a wand?"

"Philip isn't using his phone to turn water into wine," I said.

"I'm not a fan of wine," Philip said. "I prefer ale when I drink."

Aunt Hyacinth wrinkled her nose. "Naturally."

"What's wrong with ale, Aunt Hyacinth?" Marley asked. "Lots of paranormals seem to like it."

"It's banal and pedestrian," my aunt replied. She smoothed her napkin on her lap. "This family has standards."

"Yes, the Rose family," Philip said. "The Muldoons aren't so eager to put on airs."

Beside me, Florian coughed. "Here we go," he muttered.

"How's the tournament going?" Sterling asked from the

opposite end of the table. "Aster seems to think it's going well other than the one issue."

"You mean the dead leprechaun, Daddy?" Ackley asked.

Aster shushed him. "It's rude to talk about murder at the table."

"It's not like we can offend him," Aspen said matter-of-factly. "He's already dead."

"Unless you think he might be eavesdropping as a ghost," Aspen said. His eyes cracked wide open. "Do you think he might be?" His blond head whipped around, searching the dining room for signs of the spirit.

"Why would he come to our family's Sunday dinner?" Hudson asked. "That's stupid."

"Hudson, don't call your cousin stupid," Linnea warned.

"I didn't call him stupid. I called his idea stupid."

Bryn rolled her eyes. "It's the same thing to a little kid."

Silver platters paraded into the room by unseen hands and I relaxed against my chair. Arguments were less likely to continue when everyone's mouths were full, except for Hudson. He'd still talk. The werewolf tendencies were stronger in him than in his sister.

"Are you playing in the tournament, Grandmother?" Aspen asked. "I bet you'd win."

Aunt Hyacinth wrinkled her nose. "Digital games attract two types of paranormals—the unattractive and those without magic."

"Thank Goddess for that," Florian said. "For a second, I was worried you were going to say the poor."

"But my mom says you like to win at anyone's expense," the little wizard said and Aster quickly shushed him.

"I like to play," Philip said.

"But you're not keen on using magic," my aunt said. "I'd lump you in with the paranormals without magic."

Philip gave his brow an exaggerated pat with the napkin.

"As long as I'm not considered unattractive, I can live with that."

I decided to steer the conversation in another direction. "I saw the Tree of Bounty yesterday. I hadn't heard of it before. It's enormous."

Everyone fell silent.

Marley looked from one end of the table to the other, sensing the tension. "Is it bad luck to go there or something?"

"If that's the case, it shouldn't have been used as a hot spot for the tournament," I said.

"I didn't realize that it was included," Florian said. He shot a guilty look in his mother's direction. "I would have asked them not to."

"How do they even know about it?" Aster asked.

"It's an unfortunate part of our history," Aunt Hyacinth said. "I suppose they found it in articles on the town's past." She sniffed. "You know what they say about common sense."

"Are you going to tell us what the unfortunate history is?" I asked.

"I don't think it's appropriate dinner conversation," Aster said. She jerked her head toward the twins.

"Is it more murder?" Aspen asked. He surveyed the room. "How many ghosts do you think we can fit in here?"

"They're not solid," Ackley said. "They can just layer."

Philip cleared his throat. "I understand you have a special wizard in your life, Hyacinth. I'm sorry he couldn't join us this evening."

"Craig has a very busy schedule," she said in her usual haughty manner. "He can't simply lounge around playing games on his phone all day."

"Games are my passion," Philip said. "Everyone should have one. I highly recommend it."

"I have one," Florian chimed in. "More than one, really."

"My passion is magic," Marley said. She chugged half a

glass of chocolate milk. "I want to become an expert with herbs."

"What about you, Ember?" Philip asked. "What's your passion?"

"Pajamas," Marley said. "She loves to wear them as much as possible."

I silenced her with a look. "I don't always wear pajamas."

"That's true," Marley said. "Sometimes you like to sleep naked when it's too hot. Then you yell at me for opening the bedroom door."

The children giggled. I groaned and lowered my head. "I wouldn't classify that as a passion."

"Naked in bed?" Florian said. "You're halfway there."

"I don't know that I have a passion," I said. "I was never particularly good at anything like academics or music…or magic."

"I wasn't good at games when I first started playing," Philip said. "Took me ages to develop confidence."

Aunt Hyacinth gave me a pointed look. "See, Ember? Practice. This is why I provide you with private tutors."

"I thought that was so I don't embarrass you in public," I said.

"If that were the reason, I'd hire you a personal stylist too," my aunt said.

I glanced down at my plain black top and jeans. "What's wrong with this?"

Aunt Hyacinth sipped her cocktail. "You're asking the wrong question, darling."

"My passion is poetry," Sterling announced.

Aster nearly spit her wine all over the table.

"Since when?" Linnea asked.

"I've been tapping into my softer side," Sterling said. "I discovered that I really appreciate the period the humans refer to as the Romantic movement. Lord Byron's words are life-altering."

"You know what else is life-altering?" Linnea asked with a sharp glance at Hudson. "Deodorant."

Hudson shoveled turkey breast into his mouth, seemingly unconcerned.

"He makes me feel like I'm living in a locker room," Linnea said.

"Hygiene really isn't a topic for the table," Aunt Hyacinth said.

"You should really consider distributing a list of acceptable subjects prior to the meal," Philip said.

"An excellent suggestion, Philip," my aunt said. "I'll discuss it with Simon during our dinner post-mortem."

I balked. "You dissect the dinner afterward?"

"How else can we improve if we don't discuss the finer points?" she asked, completely serious.

"It's a family dinner, not an inaugural ball," I said.

Philip surveyed the table. "I must say, Hyacinth, it's wonderful to see this side of the family together. I'm so glad I decided to participate in the tournament."

"We're pleased you came," Aunt Hyacinth said. "When do you leave?"

Hudson laughed. "Here's your wizard hat, what's your hurry?"

"Tuesday morning," he said. "I wanted to make sure I was here for the announcement of the winner on Monday afternoon."

"Do you think you might win?" Bryn asked.

"I'm in contention, but I doubt I'll keep pace with the younger generation," Philip said. "They can get by on energy drinks and so forth, whereas I've found I need a solid night of sleep." He lifted his goblet of water. "And I wouldn't miss the chance to spend time with family."

"No, time is too fleeting," Aunt Hyacinth agreed. "You merely blink and decades have passed." She drew her cocktail to her lips. "Suddenly, you're surrounded by grandchildren and are no longer the center of the universe."

I'd never seen her so melancholy. "The two of you must have lots of stories from when you were younger," I said.

"Naturally," Aunt Hyacinth said. "Philip was raised here. He was like family before I even became a Muldoon."

Philip wore a hint of a smile. "My cousin was punching above his weight when he decided to court you. Then again, he always was an overachiever." He turned to me. "Your father was more like me."

"Why doesn't that surprise me?" I asked. He'd seemed fairly laidback to me, especially compared with other parents.

"It's so interesting to be sitting here with the two of you now," Philip said. "I could be sitting with your mother. You both bear a striking resemblance to Lily."

"We've seen her pictures," Marley said.

"Yes, the Hawthorne genes prevailed in the looks department, I'm afraid," Aunt Hyacinth said, "but I do believe Rose blood prevails when it comes to magic."

"The white-blond hair was such a dead giveaway," Philip said. "Hyacinth was judged even from afar because everyone recognized her at a glance. Spending time with her in public was like living in a fishbowl. You and Marley are fortunate that you get to walk around town incognito."

Aunt Hyacinth sipped her cocktail. "Philip, you exaggerate."

"Hardly," he said.

"Sounds about right to me," Florian said.

Thanks to Philip, I glimpsed a side to my aunt's life that I hadn't envisioned before. I often said we were minor celebrities in Starry Hollow. Well, fame had a price, even on a minor scale, and it seemed that my aunt had paid it from a young age. It explained a lot.

My phone vibrated in my purse and I discreetly checked the message. It was from Sheriff Nash.

Think I've got Benny's location.

I pushed back my chair. "Thank you for dinner, but I need to go."

Marley's face fell. "But I haven't had dessert. That's always the best part."

"Marley, you're welcome to stay here while your mother handles her business," my aunt said. She shifted her focus to me. "I assume you're chasing a story."

"You could say that." The story of who killed Clark.

"I'll bring her home after dessert," Florian offered.

I clapped him on the back. "Thanks. You're the best." I aimed a finger at Marley. "It's a school night, so no dragging your feet if I'm not back by bedtime."

"Absolutely," Florian said. "We wouldn't dream of operating outside your rules." He winked at Marley.

"Now you know how it feels," Aunt Hyacinth said, giving me a pointed look.

There was no way I was anything like my aunt. If anything, I was like my dad. I didn't have time to protest, though, not if I wanted to catch up with the sheriff.

"No worries, Ember. You're going to nail this story," Florian called after me.

"Thanks," I said over my shoulder. *But I really hope I'm going nail this killer.*

CHAPTER FOURTEEN

I MET Sheriff Nash on the edge of the woods. The full moon shone like a newly minted coin against the backdrop of the dark sky.

"You didn't need to come, Rose," Sheriff Nash said. "I can handle Benny."

"I know you can, but he's a werewolf and I don't want your pack instincts to kick in," I said.

He gave me a wry look. "Are you suggesting that I can't do my job when a werewolf is involved?"

I sank against a tree. "No, of course not. I know you're too professional for that."

A smile threatened to emerge. "Admit it. You're hoping to see a wolf in a fedora, aren't you?"

"You mean a werewolf."

"No." He pointed skyward. "I mean a wolf."

Sweet baby Elvis. Of course.

"When your cousins were planning this event, I guess they didn't bother to check the lunar calendar."

Well, this was unfortunate timing. With werewolves running amok, testosterone would be at dangerous peak levels. The players could be battling wolves on and off the game.

"Do you know if pack members applied for a permit to turn?" I asked.

"When's the last time my brother and his friends followed the town regs?"

Fair point. "Can we find them before they turn and stop them from running riot all over town?"

"I've already texted Wyatt, but I can't guarantee anything."

Then we could be navigating a minefield of wolves—and so could visiting players. "We should set up a perimeter and ward it to keep out unsuspecting paranormals."

"If you want to give it a try, feel free. I won't object," the sheriff said. "Anything to make my job easier right now."

"No promises," I said. I turned and faced the town. Magic pulsed through me before I even had a chance to summon it.

"*Defendo*," I said. I bent down and tapped the ground with my wand. White energy flared along the edge of the woods, spreading like wildfire.

I stood and saw the flash of admiration in the sheriff's dark eyes. "Pretty good, Rose. You've been practicing."

I watched the magical signature fade. "Not that much." I expected to feel a momentary drain from the creation of the ward, but I felt fine.

The sheriff regarded me. "You okay?"

"I am." I tried not to sound surprised. "Are you sure Benny's in the woods?"

"Yep. I called around the pack and asked where I could find him," he said.

"Wait. Benny's local?" That thought hadn't occurred to me.

He nodded. "I don't know him well, but I've seen him around, fedora included. I've had dealings with one of his older brothers a few times."

"Define dealings."

He smirked. "He's been in trouble here and there. Nothing serious."

"Do you think Benny is in the woods to shift?"

"I suspect so. I'm going to try to track him down before he turns. Harder to talk to a wolf, as I think you know."

"I'll come with you," I said.

Sheriff Nash gave me a sharp look. "I don't think that's wise, Rose. You know how wolves get."

"You'll be with me," I said. "I'll be fine." I wanted to hear what Benny had to say.

The sheriff's nostrils flared. "Have it your way. You always do."

As we trekked deeper into the woods, the moonlight disappeared and left us steeped in darkness. I managed to trip over several tree roots before having the wherewithal to conjure a spell for light.

The sheriff chuckled. "Sorry, I didn't think I'd need to hold your hand."

"Excuse me that I don't have your heightened senses, Mr. Wolf." I waved my wand around. "I can handle myself and I don't need any wolf genes to do it."

"I know you don't, Rose." Even though I couldn't see his face, I could *feel* him smirking. "I appreciate you helping out with the investigation. I know it's probably not how you expected to spend your weekend."

"I was covering the tournament for *Vox Populi* no matter what," I said. "I might as well make myself doubly useful. I get an article and you get a murderer." Hopefully.

"I feel like you get the better end of that deal," he said.

"Honestly, neither one of us does," I said. "Games like these aren't really my jam." Nor Marley's, it seemed. She'd quickly lost interest.

145

In the distance, a wolf howled, sending shivers down my spine.

"Stay close," he urged.

"Did we miss our window?" I asked.

"Not necessarily," he said. "I bet we've got players from out of town turning too."

"What about you? Will you turn?"

White teeth flashed in the inky black. "Not tonight, Rose. I'm on duty."

The sound of scattering leaves caught my attention. Sheriff Nash sniffed the air.

"This way," he said.

I crept directly behind him, careful not to step on the heel of his shoe. I hated when Marley did that to me.

Overhead, an owl hooted and I jumped forward, knocking into the sheriff. "Sorry," I mumbled.

He chuckled under his breath. "We haven't even seen a wolf yet."

"For some reason, that makes it worse." My body began to feel heavy and breathing became more difficult. I looked up at the giant ash tree and realized that it was the Tree of Bounty. The area seemed even creepier in the dark. The light on the tip of my wand fizzled out.

"What happened?" the sheriff asked.

"I'm not sure," I said. Something prevented me from doing the spell again—a pressure.

Footsteps thundered in our direction and I backed against the tree. The sheriff stood protectively in front of me. The feminist part of me wanted to shove him aside, but the mother in me let him act out his heroic urges for Marley's sake. No need to leave my daughter an orphan.

I peered at the approaching patches of light and realized that the thundering footsteps didn't belong to a pack of wolves but to a gang of eager players with their phones illuminated, including one werewolf in a fedora.

"Benny?" the sheriff called.

The werewolf glanced up from his phone to see us. "Sheriff Nash? What are you doing here?" He noticed me behind the sheriff and grinned. "Oh, sorry to interrupt."

"You haven't interrupted anything," the sheriff said. "We've been looking for you."

"Me? Why?" Benny was the picture of innocence.

"We need to ask you about an incident..." Sheriff Nash didn't get a chance to finish. Benny was off like a shot, darting between trees. We ran after him and I groaned when I saw the flick of a tail. Benny had decided that now would be a good time to shift after all.

I took out my wand, ready to conjure another spell, but the sheriff was too quick for me. He leaped through the air and tackled the wolf, pinning him to the ground. The wolf struggled for a moment, but eventually the fur and snout receded and Benny returned to his human form.

"Man, I lost my fedora," Benny complained.

"That's the last article of clothing I'd be worried about right now," I said.

Benny grabbed a leaf and held it over his private parts.

"Why did you run?" the sheriff asked.

"Because I thought I was in trouble," Benny said.

"For what?" the sheriff asked.

"I don't know," Benny said. "Every time you or the deputy comes around looking for my brother, it's because he's in trouble."

"Yes, but he's in trouble because he did something," I said. "Why do you think you might be in trouble? Did you do something?"

Benny looked perplexed. "No. Maybe. I don't know. That

argument with the leprechaun? I mean, we were only a little disorderly. I didn't think anyone would report it."

The sheriff flicked a glance in my direction. "Do you know the leprechaun's name?"

"Yeah, Clark. Smug little guy. Always posting his screenshots online like he's the gods' gift to gaming."

"What was the argument about?" I asked.

The sheriff helped Benny to his feet and Benny was careful to keep his leaf in place.

"He took a scythe and I had to wait for the supplies to replenish before I could get one," Benny said.

"What's so bad about waiting?" I asked.

"You don't understand," Benny said. "It's the principle. The dude has no etiquette." The werewolf paled. "Hang on. I heard…" He clamped his mouth shut and shook his head.

"Benny?" I pressed.

He wagged a finger. "No way. I'm not talking. I know what happened."

"You know what happened to Clark?" the sheriff asked.

"I know the dude's dead," Benny said. "That's it."

"And you didn't think we might want to talk to you about it?" the sheriff asked.

"No, man. Like I said, it was nothing. I'd forgotten about it and when I heard he was dead, I just…" He trailed off and averted his gaze.

"You just what?" I asked.

"I said good riddance, okay?" He stamped his foot. "Doesn't make me look good, does it?"

"Not really," I said. But it didn't mean he was guilty of murder either.

Benny shivered. "I'm getting chilly. Could I maybe find my clothes?"

"First, I want you to tell me where you were between five and six yesterday morning," Sheriff Nash said.

Benny's eyes rolled upward. "That's early. I was asleep."

"You weren't awake for the tournament?" I asked.

"I'm not that into it," Benny said. "I only joined because it's local and some of my friends play."

"You're out here in the dark playing," I said.

He shrugged. "That's fun. I don't care about winning."

"Can anyone verify that you were home in bed during that time?" the sheriff asked.

"My mom and dad," Benny said. "You know them pretty well by now." He grinned. "Pretty soon, they'll be having you over for family dinners."

The sheriff hooked a thumb over his shoulder. "Go find your clothes. I'm going to talk to your parents at a respectable hour in the morning. Don't even think about leaving town until I've cleared you."

Benny snorted. "Where am I going to go? I live at home and I work part-time. I don't even have my own set of wheels." He brushed past us and began hunting for his clothes.

I spotted a familiar item on a bush and plucked it from the vines. "Here you go, Benny. Crisis averted." I tossed the hat to him and he caught it with his head so that he didn't relinquish the leaf. Impressive.

"Thanks for the help," the sheriff said, once Benny was gone. "I'm going to go check out the rest of the woods and make sure the wolves aren't into any trouble. Go ahead and break your ward on your way out." He hesitated, scratching his jaw. "You want me to walk you back to the perimeter? In case you get lost, not because you can't handle yourself."

"You reached your quota of heroic gestures today when you threw yourself in front of me at the tree," I said. "I'll manage to Hansel and Gretel my way out of here, but thanks."

149

A wolf howled and the sheriff heaved a sigh. "I can tell it's going to be a late night. I'd better not find Wyatt out here."

"Let me know what you find out from Benny's parents, okay?"

"Pretend I'm wearing a fedora," he said, and tipped an imaginary hat.

I laughed. "I'd rather picture you wearing a leaf." I wished I could snatch back the words the moment they left my mouth. "Crap-on-a-stick, I didn't mean it that way." Heat rose to my cheeks and I was glad my face was obscured by the night. "I only meant that the hat wasn't cool."

His low laugh rumbled in the darkness. "It's okay, Rose. You know I don't mind either way."

"I'm not picturing you with leaves or a fedora," I said, waving my hands. "I'm not picturing you with anything at all."

"Rose, you're not helping your case."

"Good night," I yelled. I stumbled forward and tripped over another root in my desire to escape both the sheriff and my embarrassment. This only made him laugh harder and I was pretty sure his laughter followed me all the way back to the perimeter.

CHAPTER FIFTEEN

THE MISTRESS OF PSYCHIC SKILLS stood on my doorstep at an ungodly hour the next morning. I'd helped Marley get ready for school and then collapsed back into bed until five minutes before my lesson.

"We have to work indoors today," Marigold announced.

"You say that like I'll object." Given a choice between physically active and lazy, I'd choose lazy every time.

Marigold entered the cottage, her cheeks tinged with pink. "Could I trouble you for a glass of water? I should have brought a bottle with me, but I was in a hurry."

"Sure." I hustled into the kitchen and filled a glass with water. When I returned to the living area to hand it to her, she was poised on the chair like an emperor ready to be fed grapes.

"Are you feeling okay?" I asked.

"Too warm," she said, somewhat breathless. "It'll pass."

"Hello hotness your old friend. Why don't you use magic to treat for your menopause symptoms?"

Marigold's head snapped to attention. "Stars and stones,

have you lost your mind? Don't say the 'm' word out loud in mixed company."

My head swiveled, thinking that Alec or Florian had ninja-ed their way into the cottage, but there was no sign of either one. "What mixed company?"

She motioned to the Yorkshire terrier, snoring quietly on the sofa. "Him."

"You're embarrassed that the ancient dog might know about your menopause?"

She jerked a finger to her lips. "Ember, please. The more you say it out loud, the worse it is."

"You know that's not how menopause works, right? It's not a demon that gets summoned."

"Isn't it though?" She exhaled dramatically. "I've tried all the charms and potions the coven recommends, but nothing helps. I swear the recipes were created by wizards."

That wouldn't surprise me. "I guess it's one of those natural parts of life that magic doesn't allow us to mess with permanently."

"Probably the reason I was never able to improve my looks when I was younger." Marigold smoothed her hair. "I used to try all kinds of spells to make myself taller or my butt bigger, but nothing worked long-term. Just goes to show you that you can't mess with perfection."

I squinted at her. "You wanted to make your butt bigger?"

Marigold stood and aimed her bottom in my direction. "I've added more cushion naturally over the years, but it used to be a mere husk of a butt. I would sit down and get an instant muscle cramp because there was no fat to protect me from the hardness of the chair."

"That sounds...painful." *For me to hear.*

"I wish I'd had this butt my whole life. It's what my younger self dreamed of." The witch grimaced. "And now the cruel irony is that I'm too old to enjoy it."

"You're too old to enjoy your butt?"

Marigold grabbed a pillow and hugged it against her chest. "I still do okay with the men, but my younger self would've benefited greatly from my current bottom. I don't have the same energy level that I used to."

I found that hard to believe. Marigold was a sergeant cheerleader on speed as far as I was concerned. On the other hand, I didn't want to delve into the details of her dating life. Not until I had the right spell to ward off nightmares.

"Age is relative," I said, in an effort to sound diplomatic. "You're only as old as you feel."

"Tell that to the old witch I see in the mirror," Marigold shot back. "Sometimes I catch a glimpse of my reflection and think some old woman's broken into my house."

"To steal what—your sensible shoes?"

Marigold glanced down at her orthopedic tennis shoes. "I have high arches. I need the support."

"What psychic activities do you have in mind for me today?" I asked. "I definitely don't want the power to read minds while these tournament players are in town." I had a feeling their pubescent thoughts ranged from the best way to urinate without stopping the game to the challenges of dating a mermaid.

"I thought we'd practice telekinesis today," Marigold said.

I wagged a finger at her. "You're very clever," I said. "Tapping into my lazy powers."

"Yes, I thought it might appeal to you."

I raised my hand. "Can we really practice from the comfort of the cottage? I don't feel like tossing sticks around in the woods today, not with the tournament in town."

"And a killer on the loose, from the sound of it," Marigold added.

"Hey, there's a thought. Why don't you teach me to lift

153

something useful that I can use as a defensive weapon?" I said. "Maybe a sledgehammer?"

"Yes, because you're so likely to have a sledgehammer within sight when you've been cornered by a killer."

"Clark was killed with a cast iron skillet," I said.

"Yes, in a kitchen," Marigold reminded me. "Where do you expect to be within proximity to a sledgehammer?"

"Fine," I huffed. "How about I practice flipping a table Jersey style? Odds are good I'll be within range of a table."

Marigold stroked PP3's head and the dog continued to snooze. If it weren't for the steady snoring, I'd be checking his vital signs.

"I think you're overreaching," Marigold said. "You can't go from moving pencils to flipping tables. You need to work up to it. I think we should stick with sticks." She laughed at her own joke.

I glanced helplessly around the cottage, searching for appropriate items to move with my mind. My gaze landed on the desk against the wall where Marley's colored pencils were arranged in a metal cup.

"I guess a pencil can be a weapon," I said with a deep sigh. "I've seen John Wick enough times."

Marigold clapped her hands in a way that made her sound both enthusiastic and efficient. It was a gift. "Perfect. I suggest you start by actually getting up from the sofa. It's like singing, better to be in an upright position with your diaphragm engaged."

I balked. "What kind of kink are you into?"

Marigold approached me and pressed my abdomen. "Here, gutter brain. You need to tighten your core and concentrate."

"If I'm about to be bludgeoned with a skillet, I don't know that I'll be tightening anything." Maybe just my butt cheeks but that would be purely out of fear.

"You should really be practicing your skills outside of lessons," she said.

"Yes, I'll add that to my list right after laundry, mealtimes, my job, my other lessons, and my personal relationships."

Marigold put her hands on her hips. "You're never going to reach your potential if you don't practice."

"I can live with that." Whether Aunt Hyacinth could live with that was another story. "I'm going to try and lift one of the pencils out of the cup. Will that make you happy, task mistress?"

"Which color?" she asked.

I glared at her. "Seriously?"

"Choose the specific pencil in advance," she said. "That's how you hone your skill."

"Fine, I'll move the purple one." I rolled my neck from side to side and prepared to focus.

"Remember to feel the energy inside you and pour it into a ball that you can control."

I shushed her. "I can't concentrate with you babbling in my ear. It's distracting."

Marigold pretended to zip her lip and took a step backward. I zeroed in on the purple pencil. I let the magic flow through me and focused my will. Every time I thought I'd connected to the item, I found myself distracted by another color.

"They're too close together," I complained. "Can we move the purple one onto the desk by itself?"

Marigold's brow lifted. "You're asking to cheat?"

"How is that cheating? I'm practicing. Shouldn't we start easy and get harder?"

"It's a single pencil. Ember. We're already starting easy." She examined my posture. "You're too tense. You need to relax."

155

"Which is it?" I demanded. "Am I tightening or relaxing?" I shimmied my shoulders in an effort to relax the muscles.

"How about music?" she asked. "Do you think that might help or will it distract you?"

I chewed my lip. "What kind of music?"

"Classical?" she suggested.

"No, that'll put me straight into a coma," I said. "I need something in between Sleeping Beauty and The Red Shoes."

Marigold surveyed the cottage, hands on hips. "What about one of those human world musicians you're so fond of? William Joel? Bruce Springshine?"

"Yes, let's go with that," I said. "*Thunder Road* might work." It wasn't as energetic as *Born to Run* but also not as sleepy as *I'm on Fire*. I pulled out my phone and started the song.

Marigold listened intently, as though trying to absorb the music. "Okay, maybe I can see the appeal."

I arched an eyebrow. "You need to rustle up a little more enthusiasm or this lesson is over." I shook my hands to loosen them and fixated on the purple pencil. I focused my will as the music washed over me. The top of the pencil began to wiggle and I increased my concentration, tugging on it. It lifted slightly before dropping back into the container. My shoulders drooped as I turned toward Marigold.

"Stop looking like you just lost your matching sock in the dryer," she scolded.

"No," I said. "That warrants this expression." I straightened my shoulders and produced a pout. "This posture is more in line with I finished the bottle of wine, there's no more left in the house, and the stores are all closed."

"A serious problem," Marigold agreed. "If you plan ahead, however, one that's easily avoided."

I blew a raspberry at her. "Let me try again." I refocused, blotting out everything except the purple pencil. The magic flowed from my core to my fingertips and toes. I pictured the purple pencil rising and leaving all the other colors behind. This time, it kept going and floated completely out of the metal container until it was levitating about a foot above the desk. Then I turned it on its side and flew sideways in a rapid motion. The point of the pencil stuck in the wall. I faced Marigold with a triumphant smile.

"Well done, Ember." She jiggled my arm with a bright smile. That was the thing about Marigold. She appreciated my successes and didn't even mind when I gloated, unlike Hazel who would've found a way to undermine my minor accomplishment.

"Thanks," I said, flopping onto the sofa. My phone vibrated and I swiped it closer to my face.

"Uh oh," Marigold said. "Looks like someone will be needing her reading glasses soon."

I ignored her and read the text from the sheriff. "Benny's alibi checks out."

"Still no murderer then?"

"No. We found him at the Tree of Bounty last night and he ran off like he was guilty…" I stopped. "Hey, I bet you can tell me."

"Whether he's guilty? No idea, but you just said his alibi checks out."

"No, I'd like to know about the Tree of Bounty," I said.

Marigold recoiled. "Why? Are you writing an article on it?"

"Yes," I lied. "Alec thought a little controversy might sell a few more papers." That seemed sufficiently vague enough to make sense.

Marigold shuddered. "I used to have nightmares about that tree as a little girl. Even now, I avoid it on my nature walks. It's far too creepy."

"What happened there?"

"I can't believe your aunt hasn't mentioned it," Marigold said.

"Every time I've brought it up, everybody clams up, and both times I've been there, I've felt a strange sensation."

She rubbed her neck. "The hairs on the back of my neck are tickling me just talking about it."

"I felt heavy, like gravity was working overtime," I said. "And a horrible sense of dread."

Marigold regarded me curiously. "How interesting."

"Why? That hasn't happened to you?"

"Well, I wouldn't know," she said. "As I said, I steer clear of the area. I don't want to be anywhere that witches were hanged."

Her revelation shocked me. "Like they were in Salem?"

"Different reasons, of course. Everybody knew ours were actually witches. That wasn't up for debate."

"Why would witches be hanged in Starry Hollow? They practically run the town."

"Powers ebbs and flows over the years," Marigold said. "This happened during a period when the coven was weak. Many towns have a dark period of history that they prefer to ignore. The Tree of Bounty is one of ours."

"Why would witches have been persecuted in a paranormal town?"

"They were guilty of insanity," Marigold said.

I gripped the arm of the sofa. "They were executed because of mental illness?"

"I'm not even sure that they were actually insane," Marigold said. "The records were destroyed, but rumor has it that they were simply witches speaking their mind at a time when others wanted to silence them."

"How many were killed?"

"Seven," Marigold said. "Including two sets of sisters."

My stomach churned. "That's awful. No wizards?"

"No."

"They basically used murder as a tool to oppress women," I said.

She looked down her nose at me. "Why do you think no one likes to discuss it?"

Unbelievable. Paranormals weren't so different from their human counterparts after all.

"Did this happen before or after Ivy Rose was forced to step down as High Priestess?" I asked.

Marigold licked her lips, thinking. "This was decades before."

In a way, Ivy was fortunate to have only been stripped of her power when she could have been executed like the other witches.

"I can't believe the energy at the tree is still so powerful after all this time," I said. I thought of the ritual my cousins and I had performed at Palmetto House after Clark's murder. "Didn't the coven ever perform a cleansing spell to get rid of the negative energy?"

"Not to my knowledge. I think they prefer to pretend that event never happened. It's such a shameful moment in our history."

"That's not the right way to handle a traumatic event like that!" I had the feeling that Aunt Hyacinth was among those that thought it best to sweep the 'incident' under the rug. "What you fail to acknowledge is doomed to be repeated." Or something to that effect.

"Maybe you should raise it at the next coven meeting, though I'd be careful if I were you," Marigold said. "The suggestion is liable to upset some members."

"Why? The only reason to be upset is if they were complicit."

"They may not have been, but some of their ancestors were," Marigold said.

My hand covered my mouth. I couldn't believe this had happened right here in Starry Hollow.

"From what I understand, the whole thing started with one accusation and then snowballed from there," Marigold said. "Lunacy was viewed differently back then. It was seen as more like demonic possession."

Except the witches probably weren't even insane, just outspoken.

"What about the Council of Elders?" I asked. "Did they try to intervene?"

"I believe they stayed out of the matter," Marigold said. "No one else wanted to get tangled in the mess."

"Why do groups work themselves into a frenzy?" I asked. It was sickening.

Marigold nodded. "The mob mentality can be a frightening prospect."

My thoughts turned to Ivy. "Someone starts hurling accusations and, before you know it, the pitchforks are headed your way, even when the evidence is scant." I'd thought it was human nature, but it seemed to extend to paranormals as well.

"As someone who tends to move against the current, I can see why you'd feel that way."

I hugged myself. "I don't even like concerts. Too much simultaneous clapping makes me uneasy."

"I have no fear of you turning into a sheep and following the herd, Ember."

"No, definitely not." I wasn't like Sheriff Nash either. Sometimes, he acted as a lone wolf, and other times, he acted as leader of the pack. Whatever the line was, he straddled it well. It was an admirable quality.

"I should get going," Marigold said. "I'm sure you need to prepare for Hazel's lesson."

I threw my head back and moaned in protest. "I totally forgot we doubled up today."

Marigold patted my shoulder. "I'm sorry. The schedule change was my fault. I have an appointment tomorrow."

"For a menopause-ectomy?"

She laughed. "Don't I wish? Good job today, Ember. Practice again with those pencils. Maybe next time we'll level up to a ruler."

I walked her to the door, unable to stop thinking about the executed witches. After she left, I closed the door and leaned against it for support. My fingers grazed my neck and I thanked the gods that I had the luxury of being alive right now. If I'd been around during the Tree of Bounty incident, I had no doubt I would've been hanged alongside the others. My only consolation was that I would've been cursing up a storm until my dying breath.

CHAPTER SIXTEEN

PP3 STOOD at the front door and growled, interrupting my perusal of the magazine I'd managed to snag from Psychic Deadpool's place. I had every intention of returning it—once I finished reading the articles. My gaze flicked to the clock on my phone. "It's time for my next lesson already?"

I was eager to finish with Hazel so that I go to the office and see Alec, as well as check on any developments in the investigation.

The Mistress of Runecraft bustled into the cottage with her large bag in tow. She was like a walking, talking circus. "I was about to plan my funeral out there."

"And here I thought wishing on a star was a myth."

Hazel ignored the jab. "You look bleary-eyed today. Up late with the nightwalker?"

"His name is Alec, and if you must know, my eyes are tired from looking at screens all weekend."

Hazel set her bag on the dining table. "Aren't you a little old for screen addiction?"

I glowered at her. "I'm trying to help Sheriff Nash solve a murder, thank you very much."

She settled in the chair across from me. "Oh, do you mean the leprechaun?"

"Yes, his name was Clark. He was killed in Linnea's kitchen at Palmetto House."

Hazel sucked in a breath. "I didn't realize that's where he died. I heard he was killed with a four-leaf clover."

"Replace four-leaf clover with blunt force trauma with a cast iron skillet and you'd be spot on."

"Whoa," Hazel said. "Those are very hard to replace. Takes ages to get the iron just right for cooking."

"I'm more concerned with catching Clark's killer at the moment, given that he or she is still on the loose," I said. I glanced at her bag. "Where's the Big Book of Scribbles? I was doing my hand exercises all morning in preparation."

Hazel folded her arms. "Do not mock me, Ember. I have something else in mind for today." She opened the bag and produced a display case containing different colored stones.

"Are we making jewelry?" I asked. "I don't have the best small motor skills, but I'm willing to try if it means no runecraft."

"Then it's your lucky day," Hazel said. "I thought we would try something different and talk about color magic."

I scrutinized the stones. "Color magic is a real thing?"

Hazel shot me a look of disapproval. "Of course it is. Color is essentially light and light is energy. Have you never noticed the green stone that I wear around my neck?" She tapped the necklace.

To be perfectly honest, I'd never noticed it. I was usually too distracted by her curly red hair and maniacal grin. "I assumed you wore green because you're a fan of Christmas colors," I said.

Hazel's face tightened. "I wear this green stone because I'm prone to headaches and green is a wonderful healing color. It can act as a revitalizer. It's excellent for colds and heart troubles as well." She gave me an anemic smile. "I always make sure I'm wearing it when I come here for lessons."

"Because you're afraid you're going to catch a cold?"

She leaned back in her chair. "As I said, I'm prone to headaches."

"Does it matter which kind of stone?" I asked.

"The color is most important," she said. "The one in my necklace is jade."

I examined the stones in the display case. "This one's pretty," I said, tapping another green stone.

"That's a blood stone," she said. "The common ones are green or red. Excellent for nosebleeds."

Instinctively, I touched my nose. "Well, I don't suffer from those." I touched the outside of the case. "Is that the other bloodstone?"

"No, that's a garnet. It helps with anemia or blood diseases."

"Does it only work with stones? If the color is more important than the stone, how does that work?"

Hazel appeared delighted. "Finally, a sensible question. Stones are absolutely not required. Gardenia suffers from asthma and is prone to upper respiratory infections, so she makes a habit of wearing an amber ring, but also taking a piece of orange colored glass and setting it in the window. During the time of day when the sunlight streams through that particular window, she sits in front of it for thirty minutes and aims the orange light directly on her chest area. It's one of the reasons she bought a cottage with a sunroom, so that she would be guaranteed concentrated light most days."

"That's dedication," I said. I could barely commit to taking a painkiller when I had cramps. I usually just waited to see whether they would pass without too much anguish. Mostly because I was lazy.

"I thought you might like to make a necklace out of this one," Hazel said. She pointed to a pretty purple stone. "It's an amethyst."

"Will it make me better at runes?"

"If only there were a color for that," she lamented. "No, this one serves as an antidote for too much alcohol." She flashed a demonic smile. "Obviously, I thought of you."

Hardy har. I ignored her and focused on another green stone. "That one's interesting. Is it jasper?"

"No, this one is chrysolite. It's good for warding off nightmares."

My brow lifted. "That might be a good one for Marley. Is it possible to buy one at the jewelers in town?"

"I'm sure there are several shops in town that you can try," Hazel said. "I'd offer to let you have this one, but it's also good for fevers so I prefer to keep it."

"That's fine. I wasn't trying to finagle it from you. What about menopause?"

"A little soon for that, isn't it?" she asked.

"Not for me," I said. "For Marigold. Is there a stone for that?"

"A couple of choices. Ideally, she would place the stone on the affected area for a minimum of thirty minutes a day," Hazel said. "In the case of menopause, placing it over the uterus on the abdomen would suffice."

I cringed. "What would you do for urinary problems?"

Hazel folded her hands primly on the table. "There is a method to address every affliction."

Ugh. I didn't want to think about what that method might be.

"Have you noticed some of the older witches wearing turquoise?" Hazel asked.

"Is that for rheumatism or something?"

"No, it promotes youth."

"If Calla is decked out in turquoise, I'm not so sure that this is something I'm willing to believe in."

"The healing properties exist whether you choose to believe in them or not," Hazel said. "Chromapathy has existed long before you and will continue long after you're gone."

"Whew. That's reassuring. It was going to keep me up at night. I guess I'd need the stone for insomnia. Which one is that?"

"A diamond," Hazel said. "And I doubt you'll be getting one of those anytime soon."

"Meow," I said. "I don't need a diamond. I'm not even sure that I ever want to get married again."

"I suppose that's easy to say when you've already been married," Hazel said.

It never occurred to me that Hazel was bitter about not finding a life partner. "Oh, come on, Hazel. All those available wizards at the monthly coven meetings and you haven't managed to land yourself one?"

Hazel averted her gaze. "I'm not looking for your sympathy. Let's get back to chromapathy."

"Let's get back to your romantic life because that's just as likely to happen as a garnet healing my insomnia."

"This is part of your problem," Hazel said.

I leaned back and folded my arms. "And what problem would that be?"

"You're not a believer."

"How can I not be a believer? I was literally transported from the human world in a blaze of magic."

"Then why is it so outlandish to suggest a semiprecious stone can have healing properties?" Hazel asked. "There's no end to what magic can do, Ember. Jewels, flowers, runes. They can help us achieve even the most distant goals."

"Like youth and beauty?"

"Sure, why not?"

"In that case, you should have a jewel on every finger and sleep on a bed of roses."

Hazel drummed her fingers on the table. "Maybe it's because you don't believe in yourself."

I balked. "Excuse me? I believe in myself plenty."

"No, your confidence is misplaced."

I thought of Sara's boastful claims versus her actual ability. Egads, I wasn't like the troll, was I? "Give me an example."

"That blue dress you wore last week." Hazel smiled as though she'd just triple-jumped me in checkers.

"What about it?" I pictured the boatneck, knee-length dress.

"It isn't flattering."

My mouth dropped open. "Of course it's flattering. I look great in blue. It's one of my best colors."

"Knee-length doesn't suit you."

I pushed back my chair to examine my knees. "What's wrong with my knees?" I held up a leg at an award angle. "Not too bony. Not too fleshy. They're Goldilocks knees!"

Hazel's eyes rolled skyward. "Your knees aren't the problem. Your calves are a little…muscular. They tend to look even more so when you're wearing a dress that length."

I inhaled sharply. "Alec said I looked stunning."

"Because Alec wants you out of the dress by the end of the evening. I have no such interest."

I resisted the urge to sulk. This was Hazel, not the Fashion Police. "I feel good about myself in that dress and now you've ruined it."

"See? Misplaced confidence."

I was pretty sure I growled, but I tried to pass it off as a cough. "So what are you suggesting? That the confidence I have in my fashion sense should be invested in my magical abilities instead?"

"Maybe." She jerked her head toward the kitchen. "And maybe in some other areas as well."

"I'm a *terrible* cook," I said.

"Yes, and that's what you tell yourself every day, I'm sure. What if you stopped accepting that identity and started to believe that you could be a tremendous cook?"

Laughter erupted from the staircase and Raoul appeared, dragging a statue behind him. With each step, there was a corresponding thump as the head of the statue hit the stairs on the way down.

Bozo the Psychotic Clown thinks you can master culinary skills? Now I've heard everything.

"Why does your familiar have his mouth open?" Hazel asked. "Is he having trouble breathing?"

"He will be in a minute if he doesn't stop talking," I said.

Raoul tossed down the statue and it skidded across the floor and stopped at my feet. Upon closer inspection, I saw that it was the god Pan and he was—shall we say—visibly happy. Perhaps he'd spotted an attractive nymph in the forest.

Hazel stood up to peer over the table. "Why on earth has your familiar got that?"

I arched an eyebrow at him. "Another gift, huh?"

I want to stop accepting gifts. I think I'm getting the raw end of the deal.

I glanced at the evidence of Pan's excitement and cringed. "I think *I'm* getting the raw end of the deal."

"Would you mind getting rid of that so we can continue our lesson?" Hazel asked. "I can't work under these conditions."

Keep that thing here, I told Raoul. *It's working better than a charm*. Who needed a red stone when I had horny Pan?

Hazel began to gather her belongings and stuff them hastily into the bottomless bag. "I think we've done enough for today. Why don't you think about a few ailments you'd like to heal and next time we can make a bracelet?"

PP3 suddenly bolted past her, barking wildly.

"What is it, buddy?" I didn't hear the sound of a car or even a knock. The Yorkshire terrier raced back and forth in front of the door and continued to bark angrily. I crossed the room and opened the door to peer outside. There didn't seem to be anyone in sight. The dog trotted past me and began to sniff loudly, prompting me to look down.

"Great popcorn balls!" I leaped back at least foot. On the doorstep was half a pizza covered in ants. This wasn't in good shape like the kind Raoul had been bringing from the dump. This pizza had been partially eaten and seemed to have been exposed to the elements for a few days. PP3 tried to lick the crust and I nudged him back with my foot.

Hazel hopped over the pizza box without looking down. "Whatever it is, I don't want to know. I'll see you next time, Ember."

I closed the door and whirled around to call my familiar.

Raoul, where did you go? I asked.

The kitchen door opened and the raccoon scrambled into the living room. *You rang?*

I frowned. "What were you doing in there?" I squinted at his face. "Did you get into chocolate that quickly?"

He rubbed his cheek. *That's just my fur. What's the emergency? Did you forget how to operate the electric toothbrush again?*

"That never happened," I said. "I think someone left you a present on the doorstep."

He dropped to all fours and ambled to the door. He stopped and sniffed the air. *I smell pizza.* He worked the door handle and stuck his head outside. Just as quickly, he snapped his head back and slammed the door shut.

I watched him with interest. "Some gift, huh?"

He leaned against the door. *I don't think it was meant to be a present.*

"You think?" I couldn't resist the sarcasm.

Did you see who left it?

"No, but PP3 didn't like whoever it was."

He scrambled to the window and parted the curtains to look outside. *I don't see anything except Hazel on her getaway broom.*

"I don't think they planned to stick around for credit. Presumably, this is a message of some kind."

The raccoon turned to face me. *I think I might have upset someone.*

"How? By taking their pizza and donuts?" To be fair, that would be enough to upset me.

I told you I've been helping out animals down at the dump, he said. He ambled to the sofa and climbed onto a cushion.

"Yes. Why would that upset someone?"

Raoul gave me a sheepish look. *My popularity has soared for a reason. I've sort of been granting favors.*

I eyed him suspiciously. "What kind of favors?"

Barry—that's one of the beavers—he needed special wood for his dam from a different part of the forest. Raoul motioned with his paws. *So I arranged for him to get some.*

"Why couldn't Barry get his own wood?" I pictured a beaver with a leg in a cast or some other obstacle.

The part of the forest where that particular type of tree is located might belong to someone else.

I tapped my foot impatiently. "Spit it out, Raoul."

Raoul released a breath. *Fine. It belongs to Gilbert the Goat.*

"Is Gilbert an actual goat?" I asked.

What else would he be?

I crossed my arms. "And what else is Gilbert? Why does a goat have a stranglehold on part of the forest?"

The forest is divided into sections, Raoul said. *I might have crossed into Gilbert's one too many times when granting my favors.*

"Is that where you got the wood for my altar?"

His hangdog expression said it all.

I jerked my thumb toward the doorstep. "And that's Gilbert's way of expressing his displeasure? What's next? Am I going to find *you* covered with ants on the doorstep?"

I'd had my own unpleasant experience with the mob. Jimmy the Lighter was the whole reason Marley and I were in Starry Hollow now. He'd tried to kill us and might have succeeded if my cousins hadn't shown up in time.

"Why don't you stop granting favors? Or at least stop granting the ones that involve crossing Gilbert the Goat?"

Raoul snuggled against a pillow. *I don't think it's right that he claims ownership of any part of the forest. That type of tree should be available to any beaver that needs it.*

I joined him on the sofa. "I appreciate your willingness to help the little guys, but it's getting too dangerous. I can't have Gilbert and his cronies lurking outside Rose Cottage. What if something bad happened to Marley or PP3 because of this?"

Raoul picked at an imaginary thread on the pillow. *It's been really nice feeling needed. These little guys are relying on me and you see how appreciative they are. It feels really good.*

I patted his furry leg. "I bet it does." On the one hand, I understood Raoul's desire to help. On the other hand, I'd escaped that kind of danger in New Jersey. Although I wasn't convinced Gilbert the Goat was in the same league as Jimmy the Lighter, I wasn't keen to be proven wrong. And I hated ants.

That pizza was a warning, Raoul said. *If I don't stay off his turf, he's coming after me.*

I contemplated the issue for a moment. "What if there was a way we could reclaim the forest for all the animals?"

Raoul made a garbled sound. *You mean force Gilbert to give up his turf?*

"Basically, yes. He has no right to any part of the forest. It's public property."

How would you convince him? With magic?

"I could try a ward of some kind, but I'm not sure how it would work. That would keep animals out rather than allow anyone in."

Raoul set the pillow aside. *I can think of another option.*

"What is it? Anything I can help with?"

The raccoon stared at me with his beady dark eyes. *All the animals have one fear in common.*

"Really? What's that?"

One word—aunt.

I scoffed. "I don't think so, buddy. They just delivered a colony of them right to our doorstep."

The raccoon shook his head. *No, not a-n-t. Hyacinth. Your aunt.*

Ah. That made more sense. "You want me to call in the big wands?"

I don't think we have a choice.

I slid to my feet. "I'm heading over there later, so I'll take care of it."

Thanks, Ember. You're the best.

I winked at him. "I know." *Take that, Hazel*, I thought to myself. *Misplaced confidence, my ass.*

CHAPTER SEVENTEEN

THE MOMENT MARLEY arrived home from school, I ushered her upstairs to brush her hair and make herself presentable for afternoon tea at Thornhold. Aunt Hyacinth had decided it would be impolite not to host Philip one more time before his departure. It seemed my aunt's obsession with social mores outweighed her dislike of Philip.

"I would've thought you'd be madly trying to finish the game," I said, as Marley and I made our way onto the veranda.

Philip held up his phone. "I'm checking others' progress, but I fell too far behind to have any hope of winning."

Simon offered me cup and saucer. "With extra milk and sugar, just the way you like it, Miss Ember."

Florian came over to examine my cup. "It's not really tea at that point, is it?"

"Nope. Just fat and sugar, my two favorite food groups." I blew the steam off the surface of the tea before taking a sip. I'd learned my lesson after scalding my tongue once—or maybe three times. Apparently, it took me multiple times to learn my lesson.

Marley eyed a tray of homemade cookies. "Can I have one, Mom?"

"You may have two, in fact," Aunt Hyacinth said. "How was school?"

"Great," Marley said. "I turned my lab partner into a frog."

I whirled around and nearly spilled my tea in the process. "You did what?"

Marley laughed. "Relax. It was part of the lesson."

"And how are you finding your wand?" Aunt Hyacinth asked. "I hope having such a treasured family heirloom helps unlock your potential."

Marley shot me an anxious look and I knew she was worried about revealing our progress. "I love it. It's so different from everyone else's."

"Aster and I are going to the beach soon to announce the winner of the tournament," Florian said. "Will you be covering that for the paper?"

"Yes, definitely," I said.

Florian pinned me with a hard stare. "And will you be covering anything else in your article?"

"If you're worried about the murder, don't be. Another suspect's alibi checked out this morning, so there's nothing to report right now."

Philip bit into a cookie. "I don't know what this says about the players involved in the tournament, but the murder didn't seem to put a damper on the event."

"The sheriff must be nervous to have everyone leave later," Florian said. "The murderer might leave town and never be caught."

"He's directed any suspects not to leave town," I said. "Of course, if none of them is the actual killer, then holding them here won't matter."

"There's the man of the hour," Alec's voice rumbled. The

vampire strode across the veranda to shake Philip's hand. "Good to see you again, Muldoon."

Philip pumped Alec's hand enthusiastically. "I'm glad you were able to stop by. It's been far too many years."

Alec snaked his arm around my waist. "I would be remiss if I didn't at least manage a cup of tea with you before you leave."

"Alec!" Marley skipped over to hug the vampire. "I didn't know you were coming."

"I assume we'll all be heading to Balefire Beach from here for the conclusion of the tournament," Alec said.

I pressed a finger into his broad chest. "You've assumed correctly."

"Alec, might I have a quick word?" Aunt Hyacinth asked. "It's a minor business matter with the paper that requires your input." She looped her arm through his and guided him into the house.

Philip produced a pipe. "I'll move to the opposite side of the veranda so as not to pollute your atmosphere."

"I'll join you," I said. "Marley and Florian seem busy anyway." My cousin was entertaining her with all the screen-shots he'd taken over the weekend. Thanks to the game's augmented reality technology, he'd managed to stake a vampire in Elixir, slay a dragon in front of a playground full of children, and cut off an eel's head with his friends in the background holding up pints of ale.

I hoisted myself onto the low stone wall as Philip placed a mix of herbs in a pipe and lit it.

"You look like Gandalf Lite with that pipe," I said.

He puffed and held the smoke in his mouth until he spoke. "Your grandfather had a long white beard. I like to think that someone in the human world caught a glimpse of him long ago and decided to write about him."

"I guess you knew a lot of my family members."

Philip wore a vague smile. "No need to be shy, Ember. If you wish to ask me about your parents, this is your chance."

"Nobody ever talks to me about my parents," I said. "Not unless I push for a conversation."

"I can't say it surprises me," Philip said. "The family has always been somewhat rigid in their approach to emotions."

"Why?" I asked. "And how did you escape it?"

He shrugged. "I moved away." He eyed me over the pipe. "I suspect your father's intentions were similar."

"I think he was more motivated by the death of my mother," I said, "but he definitely wanted to get out from under the influence of the family."

Philip offered me his pipe, which I politely declined. "How was your father's behavior in New Jersey? I've often wondered if it made a difference to your upbringing. Was he affectionate? Did he encourage you to express yourself?"

I gazed at the blue sky above, pondering the question. "I used to think we were close, but there were so many lies."

"You must've sensed a wall of some kind, don't you think?" Smoke in the shape of cotton balls puffed from his mouth. "Maybe that's why you're so comfortable with Alec."

I squinted. "What do you mean?"

"Well, I don't know him well, but it's been my impression that the vampire is somewhat closed off on an emotional level. So maybe that's why you're drawn to him—because it feels familiar and comfortable."

"You think I'm dating Alec because of my relationship with my dad?"

He shrugged. "It's a theory. Many partners are chosen based on parental relationships. It's nothing new."

I let the suggestion settle. "So, by the same token, do you think I might be *un*comfortable with someone who displays genuine emotion and expresses their feelings?"

"Absolutely, not because you don't want it or don't deserve it, but because it feels foreign to you."

My thoughts flickered to the sheriff, how open and willing he'd been to forge a relationship with me, whereas Alec was withdrawn and buried himself in work in order to avoid real feelings. And yet I'd still chosen Alec.

"If you're right, what does that mean?" My voice came out a whisper. "Does it mean my relationship with Alec is unhealthy?" And why did a pipe-smoking, game-obsessed wizard come up with this mind-blowing theory instead of a professional therapist?

"That's not for me to say."

"My father loved me," I said, a little more insistent than necessary.

"I don't doubt that for a second, Ember," Philip said. "He took great pains to protect you—to raise you away from what he probably considered to be a toxic environment."

I angled my head to look at him. "Do you think it's toxic now?" I didn't feel that way about Starry Hollow. I loved it here, and so did Marley.

"It feels different now, I'll say that much," Philip said. "It could be due to a new generation of Rose-Muldoons. It could be the addition of two family members from New Jersey." He winked at me.

"Florian, Aster, and Linnea are pretty awesome," I said. "I don't know what I'd do without them, to be honest. They changed my life."

"That's great to hear," Philip said. "I had high hopes for them, but Florian…" He chuckled softly. "I mainly worried about the coddling."

"He's spoiled. I won't argue, but he's gotten a lot better just since I've been here." My cheeks burned. "That sounds like I'm giving myself credit."

Philip softly blew rings of smoke. "Maybe you should."

The smoky rings took the shape of horses and galloped away. "Maybe you've had more influence here than you realize."

"You're a gamer. You're not supposed to be insightful and good at feelings. You're supposed to be awkward with poor social skills."

He laughed. "I'm all that too." He pressed his lips to the pipe again. "I may have an unchecked interest in games, but I will say that breaking out of the suffocating bubble that is family made a big difference to my personal growth. I started to see the kind of toxic behavior I'd been a part of and it allowed me to make better choices as an adult."

"You seem very chill, Philip. I think whatever internal work you've done has paid off."

Alec's long shadow fell over us. "Apologies for that."

"No worries. Philip and I were having a moment," I said.

Alec adjusted his cufflinks in two crisp movements. "Is that so?"

Philip offered Alec his pipe. "I doubt you have anything to fear from me. I'm not half as sophisticated as a worldly talented vampire such as yourself." The wizard tapped the pipe and slid his feet to the ground. "I'm comfortable with who I am." He patted Alec on the chest. "Can you say the same?" Philip continued past the vampire and headed back to the house.

Alec shot me a quizzical glance. "Should I understand any of that?"

"Probably not. Philip is a pretty interesting guy though. I think Aunt Hyacinth has been missing out."

"I'm sure this isn't the first time," Alec said. "Sounds like you two had a wonderful conversation."

"He definitely got me thinking," I said. "He knew my parents. He said my grandfather had a dope beard."

Alec smiled. "Dope, was it?"

"I'm glad he was here," I said.

Florian waved to us from across the veranda. "I need to head to the beach to prepare. Would anyone like a ride?"

Marley's hand shot into the air.

"I wouldn't mind one," Philip said.

Aunt Hyacinth emerged from the house. "I'll sit this one out, thank you."

"Actually, I have a favor to ask you," I said. "Florian, I'll meet you all at the beach. There's something I need to take care of first."

"Can we play the game at the beach?" Marley asked. "I want to have the ocean as the background in one of my screenshots."

"Sounds good to me," Florian said.

Alec squeezed my hand. "Am I needed for this favor?"

"No, you're free to return to your rabbit hole."

He gave me a quick kiss on the lips. "Dinner tonight?"

"I'd like that."

I waited for everyone to vacate the veranda before I told Aunt Hyacinth what I needed from her. I didn't want to embarrass Raoul by blabbing in front of everyone. Although she agreed, I could see the skepticism in her eyes.

I hurried home to rendezvous with Raoul and put on my hiking boots. My aunt met me outside the cottage and we began our trek into the woods.

"I cannot believe you've convinced me to partake in this lunacy." Aunt Hyacinth held up the hem of her kaftan as she stepped over another fallen log.

"It's for the greater good," I said. "Peace in our time."

"We're talking about squabbling forest animals," she said. "It's absurd."

"They're part of nature," I said. "And our coven has a duty to the natural world in this town."

"Not when they're acting like fools," she muttered. "Where exactly is this Gilbert the Goat?"

"I'm not sure, but Raoul said to meet him by the retention pond."

Aunt Hyacinth's upper lip curled. "Retention pond? We're not even meeting at a natural pond?"

Only my aunt would be snobby about the type of pond involved in a meeting with the forest mafia.

"We should've ridden in on horses for the intimidation factor," I said.

Aunt Hyacinth gave me a withering glance. "I don't need an intimidation factor. I think you'll find I'm more than enough."

I didn't argue with that. "Sorry, if I'd realized how far it was, I would've had Simon bring you in that weird carriage." All the towering trees made flying broomsticks difficult.

"I'll be discussing this issue at the next meeting with the Council of Elders," she said. "We cannot have woodland creatures running riot in Starry Hollow."

"Will they actually care enough to do something about it?" I asked.

She stopped walking and looked at me. "Ember, the Council of Elders took care of this town long before you arrived and we will continue to take care of it long after…"

I laughed. "You expect me to be gone before you? Do you know something I don't?"

"I meant the council, not me specifically." She continued walking in silence until we arrived at the pond. "I see the goat. To be fair, I smelled him first."

I surveyed the area. "Where's our interpreter?"

My aunt sniffed. "I'm a witch, Ember. I don't need an interpreter." She produced her wand and waved the tip in a circle as she muttered the incantation.

Gilbert the Goat trotted forward. "It's an honor to meet you, descendant of the One True Witch."

I raised a finger. "I'm a descendant too."

The goat observed me coolly before returning his attention to my aunt. "My family is in awe of your talent. We appreciate you agreeing to this meeting."

I glanced over the goat's head and the animals assembled behind him. There were squirrels, mice, and a fox.

"It's nice to see blended families," I said.

Aunt Hyacinth looked at me sideways. "Do I need to conjure a spell to silence you?"

I sealed my lips and stood quietly by her side.

"I understand you're acquainted with the woodland bandit that's been trespassing and stealing from my property," Gilbert said.

"That woodland bandit is the familiar of my niece," Aunt Hyacinth said. "And I'm not certain what you're defining as *your* property. The last time I checked, this forest was regulated by the town but owned by no one." She took a step closer to the goat. "Or perhaps I have been misinformed." She tapped the end of her wand rhythmically against her open palm.

The goat took an unsteady step backward. "I've been, you know, in charge of this area."

"Under whose authority?" she asked. The power in her voice was unmistakable. I involuntarily shuddered and it wasn't even directed at me.

Gilbert opened his mouth and bleated. The other animals cowered behind him.

Aunt Hyacinth cupped a hand to her ear. "I beg your pardon, Gilbert. I didn't quite catch that."

"Mine," he said, in a way that would convince no one.

"As it happens, this forest falls under my domain," my aunt said. She held out her wand and I watched in amazement as it extended into a staff. She jammed the end of the staff into the ground. "Mine."

"Capisce?" I added for good measure.

Gilbert and the woodland creatures jerked their heads up and down, too rattled to speak.

"If I hear of any further issues regarding boundaries or turf," Aunt Hyacinth said, "I shall pay you a visit." She sauntered closer to him, clutching the staff in both hands. "Trust me, my dear. You do not want me to pay you a visit."

"And you leave Raoul alone," I said, shaking an angry finger for good measure. "He's been trying to show kindness to the others while you've demonstrated nothing but selfishness. Try to learn something from him instead of trying to keep him in line."

Gilbert bleated again. Then he turned and trotted through the forest with the other animals scampering behind him.

I waited until they'd disappeared from view to speak. "What kind of goat lives in a forest?" I asked.

Aunt Hyacinth shrugged. "This is Starry Hollow, darling. You share pizza with a rabid animal on a regular basis."

"Raoul isn't rabid."

"Then why do I see him foaming at the mouth so often?"

"That's not foam," I said. "That's whipped cream. He likes to make a mustache and beard with it and then try to lick it off."

She made a sound of disgust. "Yes, a raccoon familiar surely comes from your mother's side of the family."

"Philip thinks it's because I'm powerful," I said. "He said cats are lazy and selfish and don't make good familiars."

"Philip is lazy and selfish and doesn't make a good wizard," my aunt snapped.

I let her reaction roll right off me. "He seems content not to be a good wizard. In fact—dare I say it—he seems downright happy."

"If you think such a life would suit you, feel free to return to New Jersey at your earliest convenience." Aunt Hyacinth started to walk back through the forest.

I hurried after her. "You know I have no interest in that. I love it here."

She cut a quick glance at me without slowing her pace. "Are you certain? Sometimes I wonder."

"How could you wonder? Marley and I have a beautiful home here. I have a good job and an incredible boyfriend." I drew a breath as I continued to hustle beside her. "And we have family, which we've never really had before."

When we reached the grounds behind Rose Cottage, she stopped walking and faced me. "Family has always been of the utmost importance to me, Ember. It's the reason I never stopped searching for you. That's why the moment the cloaking spell was undone, I was able to find you."

"I know."

"I would do anything for family and I'd like to think that they would feel the same."

I felt like she was getting at something specific, but it was hard to know with Aunt Hyacinth. "Family looks out for each other."

"I'm glad we agree on that score." She hiked up her kaftan and carried on walking.

"Thank you for your help," I called after her. I didn't try to catch up. My aunt clearly had no intention of waiting for me, so I slowed my pace and returned to the cottage to change out of my boots for the beach.

Raoul practically jumped on me when I entered. *How'd it go? Am I a dead raccoon walking?*

"Aunt Hyacinth sorted everything out. I don't think you'll get any more grief from Gilbert."

Raoul wiped his brow with his paw. *For a scary witch, she comes through sometimes.*

Although I agreed, part of me wondered whether my aunt

had a more selfish reason for helping out. Our little exchange at the edge of the forest made me think that I was now in the unfortunate position of owing her a favor, and I didn't want to hazard a guess as to what that favor would be. Aunt Hyacinth was the witch version of Gilbert, except there was no one to bail me out of this one. I was going to owe her sooner or later—I just hoped that when the time came that I could afford the price.

CHAPTER EIGHTEEN

BALEFIRE BEACH WAS awash with paranormals by the time I arrived. Some players were still gaming on their phones, despite the official end of the tournament. Unfortunately, Deputy Bolan was the first familiar face I saw.

"Hey, Deputy Bolan," I said. "I guess you're in charge of crowd control."

The leprechaun grimaced. "I wish your cousins had hired a private security service to police the event. Next time, we'll insist on it."

"What's the problem? You just have to make sure the losers don't get out of hand. No geek riots."

"What's wrong about getting out of hand?" a slick voice asked.

I turned to see Wyatt Nash, Linnea's ex-husband, swaggering toward us.

"What are you doing here?" The werewolf didn't strike me as the type to play Wizards Connect.

Wyatt grinned. "I wouldn't dream of missing an opportunity to support the community."

I cocked a skeptical eyebrow. "You met a gamer girl, didn't you?"

"Roxy," he said. "A gorgeous shifter. Been a long time since I enjoyed a good bear hug."

"Somehow I doubt that," I said.

He chuckled. "I figured I'd come out here and see if I can help her find a few hot spots, if you know what I mean."

Inwardly, I groaned.

"Don't start any trouble," Deputy Bolan said. "Your brother and I have our hands full as it is with a murderer on the loose."

"The type of trouble I'm interested in won't involve the sheriff, only the handcuffs." Wyatt wiggled his eyebrows suggestively as he moved past us to mingle with the crowd.

"Where is the sheriff?" I asked.

"He took the far end of the beach," the deputy said. "We're going to meet in the middle and swap in an hour."

The sound of Florian's voice drifted across the beach. "Time for the winner," I said.

"That cousin of yours is a big fan of hearing himself talk, isn't he?" Deputy Bolan said.

"He's doing a great job of raising the town's profile," I said. "You should give him some credit."

"We're talking about hiring a second deputy," the leprechaun said. "That's what happens when you raise a town's profile."

"Are you saying there's been more crime because the tourism board has managed to bring in more visitors?"

"The number of minor offenses increases," he said. "Vandalism. Assaults. A shifter got thrown through the window of Elixir last night after an argument over the game got heated."

"It's not like these events are happening every week," I said. "Do you really think you need more law enforcement?"

Deputy Bolan spread his arms wide. "Look at the size of

this beach. It's filled with visitors and Sheriff Nash and I are the only two policing it. If something else happens elsewhere in town, that leaves one of us here. I bet we would've caught the killer by now if we weren't inundated with other duties."

"I guess I see your point. Does the town have it in the budget to hire someone? If not, I can speak to my aunt."

Deputy Bolan snorted. "You know the sheriff won't want you to do that."

"But she can speak to the rest of the Council of Elders..."

The leprechaun held up a hand. "It's our responsibility. We'll handle it without the influence of a Rose, thank you very much."

In the crowd, I noticed Marley with a few of her friends. They were holding up their phones so that the ocean appeared in the background of their screenshots from the game. The sight of them gave me an idea.

"Deputy, would you mind if I took another look at Clark's phone?" I asked. "I'm going to the office after this to work on my article and I think it would be helpful to look at some of his screenshots."

He hesitated. "I have it, but I don't want you to lose it. It's still evidence."

"I'm not going to lose it," I said. "Besides, we can just track it now that we know how."

"Good point." He pulled the phone from his back pocket and handed it to me.

I turned toward the makeshift stage to watch as Florian and Aster declared the winner.

"And the winner of the first annual Starry Hollow Wizards Connect tournament is Stuart Mackenzie, the player known as vladtheinhaler," Florian said.

Aster held up a trophy that looked like the Emerald Chalice in the game. A nice touch.

As the vampire climbed onto the stage, I manouvered

closer to the stage for a better view and to take a photo for the paper. I spotted a familiar banshee at the foot of the stage clapping wildly.

Great popcorn balls of fire. Was Nova his girlfriend? I wasn't sure which one to feel sorry for. They both seemed pretty awful. I had to admit, I was disappointed that one of the geekier players didn't win. I would have loved to see obiwandkenobi up there collecting the trophy.

I waited for Stuart to step down and the players to stop congratulating him before I approached the vampire.

"Hey, Stuart. Not sure if you remember me. I'm Ember Rose, a reporter for Vox Populi. I'd love to interview you for the article I'm writing."

He peered at me. "Front page?"

"Sure," I lied. Not like there was anything he could do about it after the fact.

"In that case, I'd be delighted. I'll meet you at your office in an hour, then I'm out of here."

"That works for me," I said. He'd better give me some positive quotes about his visit, too, or Florian would have my head.

I made arrangements for Marley to stay with Florian while I went to the office to prepare. I sat at my desk and clicked through the screenshots of Clark's achievements prior to the tournament. At first glance, everything seemed intact other than the gold and supplies that had been donated to obiwandkenobi. There was a screenshot of each victory. I recognized the backyard of Palmetto House in one shot and the interior of the Caffeinated Cauldron in another. I even recognized other players in the background. I made a list of each foe he defeated in case to help me craft the article. The vampire. The knife. The dragons. The ogre. When I finally finished the list, I frowned. Where was the magical eel that Philip had mentioned? The secret challenge that Clark had discovered. I scrolled through again. It had to be here. Clark was meticulous about his screenshots.

After my third review of the screenshots, I admitted defeat. The screenshot with the eel was missing, but why? An idea nagged at me. We'd assumed the killer wanted the phone because of Clark's prowess, but what if it was unrelated? My pulse raced as I started tapping my way around the phone. If there was something on there the killer didn't want anyone to see, then he would have deleted it before discarding the phone.

I needed to see that missing screenshot. I pulled out my wand, ready to do a spell. "Crap," I said, sinking against my chair. "No magic can be used on the game."

Suddenly, I bolted upright. But that didn't mean magic couldn't be used on the phone! The screenshot had been deleted and was, therefore, outside the purview of the game. With my heart pounding, I held my wand over the phone. I gathered my energy into a ball and released it. *"Restituere,"* I said.

The screen shimmered until an image appeared. I saw the eel first and knew I'd hit the jackpot. This was it. As the image became clearer, I scanned the picture for clues. There was only one image in the background, but it was the only one I needed. Nova was wrong. Her boyfriend wasn't with a bimbo fairy. She was a bimbo pixie. To be fair, I didn't know that Shelley was a bimbo at all. Nova's boyfriend likely lied about his relationship status. It appeared that Psychic Deadpool had been right. Nova and Stuart had no future, unless she planned to continue to date him as he served out his sentence. Some girls were into that.

I saved the screenshot to photos and attached it in a text addressed to Sheriff Nash. I smiled, imagining the sheriff's face when he received a text from Clark. I added a quick note just as the door opened and Stuart waltzed in, ready for his closeup. I hit send and slipped the phone into my purse.

"I'm here for my ten minutes of fame," he announced.

"Great," I said. "Give me one second and I'll get my questions ready." I tried to keep my hands from shaking as I began to type on the computer.

He ambled closer to my desk. "Don't take too long. My bus leaves in half an hour and I'm not missing it. My girlfriend's waiting at the station with our bags."

Oh no. I couldn't let him leave town. I had to keep him here until the sheriff arrived. I hoped the sheriff wasn't too busy with crowd control to check his texts.

I flashed a wide smile at Stuart. "How does it feel to be a winner?"

"No different from any other day." The vampire leaned over my desk, displaying his fangs. "I'm feeling generous in light of my victory. How about I let you rub me for good luck?"

His arrogance made my blood boil. "The internet is forever," I said.

"I wasn't suggesting that we record it." His lips curved. "But now that you mention it…"

Come on, Granger. Look at your phone.

"I would think you'd be worried about your girlfriend seeing it," I said. "That was your concern, wasn't it? That if Clark uploaded his images, Nova would see your canoodling session with the pixie."

His expression hardened. "I don't know what you mean."

I rolled back my chair to put distance between us. "I think you know exactly what I mean."

His body tensed. "You recovered the screenshot?"

I tried to maintain a casual air, despite the knot in my stomach. "Look, I can see the attraction. Her voice is far more tolerable than Nova's."

"The sound of dolphins mating is more tolerable than Nova's voice."

Well, there was a mental image I didn't expect to have today. "Why not break up with her? Why bring her to the tournament at all?" I asked.

"You think I didn't want to leave her behind? You have no idea what she's like." He began to pace back and forth in front of my desk. "The banshee is psychotic. She once threatened to bury me in a sealed coffin if she ever caught me cheating. I can only imagine what she'd do if I broke up with her."

"Does Shelley know you're here with your girlfriend?"

"Shelley doesn't need to know. It's not like I intend to see her after I leave Starry Hollow."

"You didn't know her before the tournament?"

"No, I met her the night we arrived after Nova had gone to bed," he said. "I made plans to play with her during the game because I knew Nova would be occupied elsewhere."

The vampire's cowardice was unreal. "So Clark had to die because you were too chicken to do the right thing?"

Stuart stopped and looked at me. "I didn't intend to kill him. I only wanted him to delete the screenshot so that it didn't end up on social media. As you said, the internet is forever and Clark always shared his screenshots. It was something he was known for."

"So you went to see him early Saturday morning?" I asked.

"I knew where he was staying. I'd tried to get a reservation there myself as it was clearly one of the better inns in town. I wanted to take care of the screenshot before the tournament began so that I wasn't distracted."

"But Clark refused?"

"Not only did he refuse, he thought it would be amusing to post the picture in the tournament chat room. He started tapping his screen and laughing." The vampire's nostrils flared. "I picked up the nearest object and hit him before he could finish."

"You didn't kill Clark to remove the competition," I said quietly.

He laughed. "No. Funny how life works out, isn't it?"

Hilarious. "Nova isn't interested in the game though," I said. "How would she have seen the screenshot?"

"Trust me, she'd see it. I've caught her stalking friends' accounts, just to see if I'm hiding anything from her." He drew a circle in the air next to his ear. "She's loco."

Slowly, I slid my hand toward my purse in an effort to reach my wand without drawing his attention. "Why did you donate the gold to obiwandkenobi's account?"

Stuart threw his head back and laughed harder. "Because the name is ridiculous. That poor sop needed a little excitement in his life, and I was only too happy to provide it."

"It wasn't personal then? You didn't have an issue with Patton?"

"No, I don't even know him. It was simply an easy way to deflect attention from me. Then I left the phone in the bushes near the ash tree because it was a hot spot with plenty of foot traffic. I knew someone would pick it up and leave their dirty prints all over it."

My fingers curled around my wand, but I kept my eyes locked on the vampire. "You would've been better off destroying the phone."

Stuart tapped the top of my computer. "Hindsight is twenty-twenty, isn't it? I'm sure you'll agree given our current situation."

"And what situation is that?"

The vampire snarled and put his fangs on full display. "Do you really think I have any intention of letting you turn me in?"

"Do you really think I have any intention of letting you go?" I continued to inch my chair backward, wishing that the sheriff would burst through the door.

"You'll let me go because you'll be dead, just like that wretched leprechaun." He shoved my computer aside and climbed onto the desk to reach me.

"Where's a sledgehammer when you really need one?" I lamented. I hated when Marigold was right. My gaze fell upon the pencils scattered across Bentley's desk. There wasn't time to worry about the right background music or whether I chose the correct pencil from the group.

Stuart lunged for me and two dozen pencils shot into the air. They flipped sideways, zooming toward him like fighter jets. Before he could react, they caught his clothing and forced him back against the wall. Their sharpened tips embedded in the wall and pinned him in place. One pencil managed to shoot through the crotch area and he howled in protest. I heard the tear of fabric and knew it was only a matter of time before I had a naked vampire attacking me.

I aimed my wand and said, "*Congelo!*"

The vampire froze and I tossed my wand onto the desk so that I could call the sheriff with my own phone.

"I'll never tell Marigold about this," I swore to myself as I waited for the sheriff to answer. I'd be practicing telekinesis on pencils for the rest of my magical life if she knew what I'd done.

"What's up, Rose?" the sheriff asked.

"I'm insulted. I sent you a text, but you didn't reply."

"I don't have a text from you. I have one from an unknown number, but I didn't read it yet."

"Read it on your way over to my office," I said. "I have a trophy on display and you need to admire it. Be sure to bring your handcuffs."

"Rose, that sounds far kinkier than you probably intend. Be there in a minute."

I set down the phone and returned my computer to an upright position on the desk. It seemed I had an article to finish.

CHAPTER NINETEEN

BUTTERFLIES SWIRLED in my stomach as I entered the headquarters of the Silver Moon coven for the monthly meeting. I wasn't typically nervous at these events, but I knew I planned to poke a hornet's nest—something that was really going to piss off my aunt.

"Ember, how delightful. I feel like I only see you once a month," Gardenia said.

"That's because you do," I replied.

"You should attend some of the intermittent coven events," Gardenia said. "We'd love to have you."

"I'm a working single mom, Gardenia. I'm lucky to shower once a day."

"Fair point." The Scribe smiled. "I saw your name under New Business. Care to offer a sneak preview?"

"I think it would be best to wait," I said.

She leaned over. "Calla thinks you might want to make an engagement announcement."

I started to choke on my saliva. "No, that's not on the agenda."

"Too bad. Some of us would love to see a vampire-witch wedding. It would really spice things up."

"You'll have to hold out hope that Florian meets a nice vampire then," I said.

Marigold intercepted me on my way to the snack table. "I see your name on the agenda. Would this have something to do with our recent conversation?"

"It would," I said. "I also brought you a little present." I dug into my purse and retrieved a tiny packet.

"A present for me?" Marigold touched her clavicle. "Whatever for?"

"For being brave enough to tell me about the Tree of Bounty." I emptied the packet into her open palm. "It's a special stone that's meant to help with menopause symptoms. Hazel calls it chromapathy and forced me to learn about it."

Marigold closed her fingers over the stone and blinked away tears. "Oh, Ember. This is so incredibly thoughtful. Thank you."

"I hope it works. You're supposed to place it over the affected area twice a day for half an hour a pop."

"I'm willing to try anything at this point." She clutched the stone to her chest. "You never cease to surprise me."

"Well, if they ever try to hang me for mouthiness, you'll be on my side, right?"

"Always."

The bells began to ring and the witches and wizards filed into the cavernous hall. I took my place at the front of the room with my family. I squeezed between Linnea and Florian, mainly because they were the two least likely to hex me after I made my public suggestion. As much as I loved Aster, she was more like her mother when it came to rules and propriety.

"You're very fidgety," Linnea whispered during the budget discussion.

"You'll understand why in a minute."

"And now for New Business," the High Priestess said. "I understand Ember Rose has something to say."

I ignored the fear coiled in the pit of my stomach and took my place in front of the coven. I took Marley's suggestion and focused on a point at the back of the room so that I wasn't looking at anyone in particular, yet I appeared to be making eye contact.

"I recently learned of the history of the Tree of Bounty," I began. As expected, a hush fell over the hall. "I know it's a difficult topic, but I think it deserves a conversation."

"You have no right to drag this back into the spotlight," a wizard called. "What's done is done."

I couldn't see who it was. "It seems to me that the tragedy was never fully acknowledged and that tree still retains negative energy from that shameful time."

"Sit down, Ember," a witch yelled.

Aunt Hyacinth rose to her feet and I prepared for her to escort me from the hall. Instead, she said loudly, "Let her speak."

With my aunt's blessing, my body relaxed. "I'd like to suggest a coven ritual to cleanse the tree and restore its good energy. When I was there, I felt like I was carrying the weight of the world. It was horrible. We owe it to those executed witches to acknowledge the wrong and disperse the bad energy."

"I don't know that we can fit it into the schedule," Gardenia said. "There are so many events coming up already…" She trailed off, her gaze darting to the High Priestess.

Iris appraised me. "Your argument has merit, Ember. I'd like the chance to discuss it…"

"Why don't we just put it to a coven vote now?" Florian called. "If it's vetoed, then nobody needs to worry about the schedule."

The High Priestess appeared at a loss. She glanced at the High Priest, who nodded.

"Very well then," Iris said. "As we're all gathered in one place, we may as well get it over with."

The witches and wizards pulled out their voting stones— white for 'aye' and black for 'nay.' Each of us stepped up to a large black cauldron and placed our vote inside. I waited impatiently while the votes were counted. Even the brownie from the snack table did little to ease my anxious mind. Finally, Iris resumed her place at the front of the room.

"It seems we'll be adding a ritual to the calendar this month," she said.

I beamed with pride. It felt good to do something positive for the murdered witches. Across the table, Aunt Hyacinth offered a nod of approval. "Well done, Ember. You're becoming quite the natural leader. I never thought it possible."

"I didn't think you'd want the ritual."

"I started thinking about the tree after you mentioned it at dinner during Philip's visit. You're right. It was a travesty of justice. I'm proud of you for raising the issue."

"Thank you," I said. I basked in the momentary glow of her admiration.

"You won me over," Linnea said. "I thought about Clark and cleansing Palmetto House and realized that it was only right for our own coven witches to be given the same treatment. If any parts of their spirits linger there, the ritual will release them and let them finally be at peace. They deserve that."

A wizard named Joseph hobbled over to me with a cane. "My ancestor was a ringleader in that fiasco," he said. "I've always felt so ashamed. I wanted to forget that moment in history ever happened."

"You're not responsible for the acts of your ancestors," I said.

"I know, but even the house I live in..." He paused. "I ended up owning that house because the witch that originally owned it was hung on the tree and so my ancestor inherited it."

"And you feel guilty," I said.

"How can I not?" He seemed thoughtful. "Perhaps I should have the house cleansed too. Even though she wasn't killed there, there must be residual negative energy. The house is an ill-gotten gain."

"It might make you feel better," I said.

He broke into a relieved grin. "I'm so glad you brought this up, Ember. I never would have had the courage to face it."

"It's deeply upsetting," I said. "I can understand why everyone wants to avoid it, but sometimes the issues we most want to avoid are the ones we have to force ourselves to confront. It's our best chance for personal growth." I had Philip to thank for that line of thought.

"Your parents would be very proud of the witch you've become," Joseph said.

My chest tightened at the mention of my parents. "Thank you. That means a lot to me."

When I arrived at the cottage, Marley was sound asleep. Mrs. Babcock gathered her knitting and started for the door.

"Just so you know, there was some noise from the kitchen earlier," she said. "I think it was your familiar scrounging for food again."

"Yes, that wouldn't surprise me," I said. "Good night, Mrs. Babcock."

I closed the door behind the brownie and spun on my

heel to investigate Raoul's shenanigans. I threw open the kitchen door and halted in my tracks. On the island was a completed altar, adorned with my grimoire, a candle, and a framed picture of Billy Joel. The picture was torn and the glass was cracked, but it didn't matter.

Raoul emerged from the pantry with my not-so-secret stash of cookies. He stopped short when he saw me. *Oops.*

I pointed at the altar. "Is that for me?"

I think it's obvious. You told me not to work on it in the house.

I walked over to admire his handiwork. The wood had been smoothed and refined. "Raoul, it's amazing. Thank you so much."

And you said I can't use tools. He snickered. *You're a tool.*

I paged through the grimoire. "We should keep some of Ivy's things on here as a way of remembering her."

Not her Book of Shadows, he said. *Not until you've come clean with everyone about it.*

I glanced at my hands. "They stopped tingling. I guess whatever magic that released has dissipated."

Or it's entered your body and altered you on a molecular level.

"I wasn't bit by a radioactive spider," I countered. "I opened a Book of Shadows."

A book created by the most powerful witch in the Rose family, outside of the One True Witch.

I blew air from my nostrils. "You're right. I can't discount Ivy's power."

Maybe this is the reason your aunt wanted access to it. That's what you suspected from the beginning.

"So far, I'm not lifting cars over my head or throwing thunderbolts. I'm not even convinced we'll have access to her magic."

From what you said, Ivy wasn't always overwhelmed by her magic. It took hold over time. The stronger she became, the harder it was for her.

And if that happened to me, would I be doomed to suffer Ivy's fate? No. The world was a different place now. The coven would be supportive. They'd try to help rather than strip me bare and boot me to the curb.

Wouldn't they?

Worry gnawed at me. I wasn't one of them in the same way Linnea and Aster were. Even though I'd been born here to parents in the coven, I'd lived in the human world most of my life. I had a child with a human partner. I was already so different. An Other. Ivy had been one of them her entire life, but it wasn't enough to save her. I thought of the Tree of Bounty and the murdered witches. It had been a different event in a different time period, but it was yet another example of a frenzied response to powerful women. Fear bubbled in my blood. I had to keep this a secret. I'd been so worried about putting Marley in danger. I didn't stop to think that putting myself in danger was a different kind risk to Marley. What would happen to my daughter if the coven turned against me? Would they turn against her too? Or would they try to take her away from me? Neither scenario was comforting.

I tried to shake the unwelcome thoughts from my mind. No, the coven was better than that. They worshipped the Roses.

Ivy had been a Rose.

I blocked any further thoughts on the subject from my mind. It was late and I was tired.

How was the meeting? Raoul asked. *Are they going to do the cleanse?*

"They are." See? Things were different now.

It's been a good week for you, Raoul said. *You caught a killer and you convinced the whole coven to wash a tree.*

I gazed at the altar—the physical representation of my life as a witch in Starry Hollow. "It has been a good week, Raoul.

In fact, it's a pretty good life." I rubbed the top of his head. "Thank you for reminding me."

That's what familiars are for. The raccoon held up the tin for me to open. *Now, how about a cookie?*

ALSO BY ANNABEL CHASE

Thank you for reading *Magic & Misdeeds*! Sign up for my newsletter and receive a FREE Starry Hollow Witches short story— http://eepurl.com/ctYNzf. You can also like me on Facebook so you can find out about the next book before it's even available.

Other books by Annabel Chase include:

Spellbound Paranormal Cozy Mysteries

Curse the Day, Book 1

Doom and Broom, Book 2

Spell's Bells, Book 3

Lucky Charm, Book 4

Better Than Hex, Book 5

Cast Away, Book 6

A Touch of Magic, Book 7

A Drop in the Potion, Book 8

Hemlocked and Loaded, Book 9

All Spell Breaks Loose, Book 10

Spellbound Ever After

Crazy For Brew, Book 1

Lost That Coven Feeling, Book 2

Wands Upon A Time, Book 3

Charmed Offensive, Book 4

Poetry in Potion, Book 5

Cloaks and Daggers, Book 6

Federal Bureau of Magic cozy mystery:

Great Balls of Fury, Book 1

Fury Godmother, Book 2

No Guts, No Fury, Book 3

Grace Under Fury, Book 4

Bedtime Fury, Book 5

Three Alarm Fury, Book 6

Hell Hath No Fury, Book 7

Spellslingers Academy of Magic

Outcast, Warden of the West, Book 1

Outclassed, Warden of the West, Book 2

Outlast, Warden of the West, Book 3

Printed in Great Britain
by Amazon